Trouble On The Kansas Plains

The search for truth about a murder requires Oli August to return to the western frontier.

James Oliver Virmala

Edition 1

Cover Photo By Tom Sherley

Copyright © 2019 James Oliver Virmala

ISBN: 978-0-9972536-4-1

FOREWORD

Many of the readers of my books have asked for more stories about Oli August. This book takes place nine years after his original adventure in the wilderness. It is my hope you enjoy spending more time with Oli as he overcomes betrayal and challenges on the Kansas plains.

CONTENTS

BOOKS BY THE AUTHOR

Oli's Gold Book One
Search For Oli's Gold Book Two
Return To Oli's Gold Book Three
To Be A Mountain Man
Trouble On The Kansas Plains
Frontier Justice
Return Of The Mountain Man
The Tall Man
The Prospector
The Green Valley
Twilight Of The Mountain Man
The Mother Lode
Quest Of The Mountain Man
Journey's End
Rufus Pike
Rufus And The Pup
The Winding Trail Home
Rufus The Lost Years
The Kankakee Kid
Bogus Island
Tyler Tomas The Brothers' War
War of 1812 The Choice

ACKNOWLEDGMENTS

To our brides, with whom we share goals and dreams and raise our families, along with facing the challenges of everyday life. After a lifetime of working and playing together, we get to relax and travel through the retirement years, still seeing the beautiful girl, woman, and partner we married so many years ago.

CHAPTER ONE

Sweat glistened on Oli's brow, matting his blond hair and dripping from his moustache, as he struggled to lash the rails to the corral posts. The strong, wet leather would shrink, creating a tight bond and work well until he replaced them with wooden pegs or metal spikes. Stepping back to survey his work, he mopped his rugged face with a neckerchief.

It was the spring of 1849. Oli was building a new corral next to the small barn. The home was on the banks of the Turkey River, near the spot where he had first met his wife, Joan. The town had been known as Pony Hollow until the past year, when the founders had re-named it Elkader.

Spring had come early to Iowa, and Oli had plans to put a porch onto their log house and expand the barn. Stakes were driven into the ground, laying out the dimensions of each. Life had been good since he had emerged from the ordeal in the wilderness. The town was growing, offering work for his woodworking skills. His broad shoulders and narrow waist were evidence of many hours of swinging an ax or sawing planks.

The sound of footsteps caught his attention. He turned to see his young son, Karl, coming down the path. The small boy had blond hair and blue eyes like his father.

"Come eat, papa," the boy said, and then turned to race his father to the house. Smiling, Oli pretended to compete with his son.

Joan stood in the doorway, watching. Her gingham dress moved with the spring breeze, showing evidence of the future brother, or sister, for Karl. Her normally smiling hazel eyes showed concern.

The house smelled of fresh-baked bread, made before the day had become too warm. The checkered cloth covered a sturdy table built by Oli. The meal included bread, churned butter, blackberry preserves, and sliced venison from the previous night's supper. A pot of hot, black coffee boiled on the new, ten-plate stove.

Already seated at the table was his daughter, Jenny. Her strawberry blond hair hung in little ringlets. She was tapping her spoon on the table, anxious for the meal to be served.

Joan served the food using tin plates and mugs. She sat across from Oli and picked at her meal. Karl, sitting on tall chair built by his father, was busy devouring bread with preserves. His cheeks were covered with the sticky blackberry.

"You aren't hungry?" Oli asked.

Joan frowned. "I'm sorry. I got some bad

news in the mail today. I wanted to wait until after the meal to talk to you about it."

Oli knew that his wife enjoyed cooking and she believed mealtimes should be a happy gathering. To go against this meant the news had to be very unsettling.

He quickly ate the last bit of meat and bread from his plate and skipped the second helping. Setting his fork on the plate, Oli adjusted his chair back a bit and took up his cup.

"Very good meal, Joan." He smiled at her and took a sip of coffee. "Now, what news did we get?"

Shooing the youngsters outside, she turned to her husband. Hesitating a moment, Joan spoke. "It was a letter from my brother, Martin, at Fort Leavenworth. He is in serious trouble." Tears welled up in her eyes.

Blinking rapidly, she continued. "He has been charged with stealing the soldiers' payroll and killing a guard."

"He did what?" The impact of the news shook Oli.

He had met Martin only once, when he and Joan were married. He was a young, sharp-looking junior officer in the army. It was just before he'd gone to Fort Leavenworth as the paymaster. Her brother was well-respected around Elkader and known as an honest man.

Joan took the letter from her apron pocket and handed it to Oli. Turning, she busied herself, cleaning up after the meal.

Quickly, Oli read the short letter. It said little

else, except what Joan had told him. There was no explanation of what had happened, only a promise that he would write again later.

Putting down the letter, he watched his wife. It was obvious she was fighting back tears. "I will go and find out what happened."

Dropping the tin plate she was washing in the dishpan, Joan ran to her husband. He had said the words she'd wanted to hear, yet feared he would say. Holding him tightly, she wept.

Feeling her swollen belly against his, Oli looked over her head at their young son, standing in the doorway and staring at them in wonder.

* * *

There was much planning to do before heading west. The baby was five months away. The midwife lived less than a mile away. Joan could take care of the garden and chickens. Their neighbor would care for the three milk cows and a horse. Oli looked at the wooden stakes as he walked towards town. The projects would have to wait until next year. With everything going well, most of the summer would be over before he returned.

Oli had a bay gelding that was in excellent condition and could carry him to Fort Leavenworth in just over two weeks. The remaining draft horse would be available, if needed, around home.

His mind was a flurry of thoughts as he walked toward the mercantile. A large man stepped out from a doorway and blocked the stone walk . . . Tate Wolfe.

"Excuse me, Tate," Oli said, attempting to step aside.

"Not so fast, August," Tate sneered. "Heard about your crooked brother-in-law."

Laughing, he continued. "I imagine you will be going there to watch the hanging."

Oli knew this was not the time to get into a fight with Tate Wolfe. He and his brother Jacob had always looked for opportunities to make Oli's life difficult, ever since he had bested them on the banks of the Turkey River and won Joan's hand.

"I don't have time for games with you today, Tate. But if you do not step aside, I will be forced to beat you and embarrass you in front of the whole town," he said, his blue eyes as cold as stone.

Tate glanced up and noticed the men still out of earshot, walking towards them.

"Not today, August. I've a meeting at the bank and don't want to show up with bruised knuckles." He then quickly turned and walked away.

Oli fought down the urge to catch up to Tate and dress him down. He could feel his face burning and the adrenaline soaring through his veins. Shaking his head to clear his thoughts, He knew there was nothing to be gained by doing so.

A slender man with a thin moustache looked up as he entered the mercantile. It was George Walters, the owner. "What can I do for you Mr. August?"

Oli handed George his list. "I have a trip to take and need a few things."

"Heard about Martin," George said, licking the

end of his pencil. "Hmm . . . lead, powder, flint, caps. You plan to go bust him out?"

"No, George." He smiled. "I do intend to go and find out what happened."

"Well, Martin was a good boy. Just doesn't sound like him." Turning to his well stocked shelves, the merchant began to fill the order.

Oli stepped outside to get some fresh air while his order was being filled. Glancing around the street, he felt a sense of pride. The town was growing and he had been a part of it the past six years. New houses and businesses lined the street. Walks of stone or wood kept the dust or mud off the shoppers.

His home in Finland seemed long ago. He now had a family in the United States and a new town that he could call home. This would be the first time he would be leaving Joan for any amount of time. Up till now he had only taken hunting trips, never lasting more than a week.

"Got some dried apples in," George called from inside the store. "Did you want some to take along?"

"Not for the trip," he called back, "but I will take enough for a couple pies for Joan."

Walking back into the store, he saw that the order had been filled. George was tallying up the last of the items on a piece of wrapping paper.

Looking up, he smiled at Oli. "I put in a little something sweet for your youngsters."

"Thanks, George. You'll be their best friend." As he handed the merchant coins to pay for the goods, Oli had a flashback to six years ago. He had come into the mercantile dressed in rags and paid for a new set of clothes with a gold Spanish coin. He remembered that the look of disdain on George's face had turned to the smile he was seeing now.

Walking home with the goods in a flour sack, Oli mused. Neither he nor Joan had mentioned the contents of the letter to anyone, yet everyone seemed to know about Martin. George Walters also handled the mail. The seal must have broken on the letter while in his care.

CHAPTER TWO

The bay, saddled in front of the house, sent out puffs of steam into the brisk morning air as it snorted impatiently. Oli sat holding a fresh cup of coffee and the children on his knees, knowing it was time to go. Joan kept up a constant, light-hearted chatter, assuring him that she would be okay. He knew it was just a front to make him not worry about her.

His cap and ball revolver was on his hip and felt awkward in the house. Oli had been ready to mount up and ride away when Joan had called out, telling him she had fresh coffee made. It had taken little encouragement to convince him to sit another moment. The coffee was hot and strong, but somehow lacked the normal pleasure.

He was heading into Indian Territory. There was also the ongoing conflict with Mexico. Odds were that neither would be problems on the trip. He dared not talk about these with Joan. The plan was to travel to the fort and meet with Martin. More than likely, he would be unable to help the situation. He would then come back to Elkader with an update for Joan, a task he was not looking forward to.

Giving Karl and Jenny a last bounce on his knee while singing an old Finnish song, Oli set them down and turned to Joan. She quit talking in midsentence and rushed to his arms.

"Oli August," she said in a scolding tone, "you come back now. You come back soon and with good . . ." Her voice broke and she cried softly.

"I will, my dear bride," he whispered. Kissing her softly and placing his hand on her belly for a moment, Oli took a deep breath and walked out the door.

The bay bobbed its head and stomped as he walked up. It left sharp indentions in the dirt from the new shoes he had had put on. After tightening the cinch and checking the saddle bags and bedroll, Oli swung into the saddle. Adjusting his flat-brimmed hat, he turned the bay up the road. Looking back a moment at the house, he waved to Joan.

As home disappeared from view, he felt a chill of realization that this could be the last time he saw his family. Men traveling the West had been lost without a trace. The pain he felt was nothing like the feeling he'd had when leaving his home in Finland. Then, there had been the excitement of seeing a new land and seeking his fortune. The heavy feeling in his heart stayed with him as he rode south of town.

He looked up, seeing a lone horseman sitting alongside the road. It was Jacob Wolfe. Momentarily, he placed his hand on the Hawken .50 in his scabbard. Changing his mind, he removed the loop from his

Paterson Colt .28 caliber. It was loaded with four balls, with the hammer resting on an empty chamber.

Riding up to Wolfe, Oli's eyes were drawn to the crippled hand. Jacob had broken the hand during their first meeting, when he'd punched at Oli's mid-section and hit his money belt filled with gold coins. The good hand was holding the reins. This was noted and Oli relaxed.

"Are you pretending to go help Martin, while sneaking off after more gold coins?" Jacob asked accusingly.

Many had speculated about the origin of the Spanish gold coins he had shown up with and it was rumored that there were many more where they'd come from.

Snorting, Oli rested his hand on the butt of the Paterson. "You spend too much time worrying about where I am going. There is no more gold for me to go after. You're welcome to join me on the trip to Fort Leavenworth. Tate will take care of your shipping business while you are gone."

The offer caught Jacob off guard. Flustered, he spurred his horse, narrowly missing the bay. Oli watched him gallop back towards town. Smiling, he turned his horse back down the road. Another time he would be pushed to deal more forcefully with the man, but today was not the day.

The goal was to travel 30 miles each day. His destination was southwest of Elkader. Fort Leavenworth was built on bluffs located on the west side of the Missouri River. It was just north and west of Independence. This was an area that Oli had traveled nine years earlier.

He carried a knife on the nape of his neck. He called it the Good Knife. A man named Wink on that earlier trip had taught him to throw the knife. Having the knife had made it possible to survive the winter of '39 in the wilderness.

Oli reflected on the previous trip. He had been ill-prepared to face the wilds of the western frontier. He had been following the dream of a dear, departed friend, Jolly, of Spanish gold in the West. This trip had a more honorable mission. Joan and the family was the most important thing in his life, and he was doing this for her.

The shadows were short in the midday sun when he stopped to give the horse a brief rest next to a stream. Oli drank upstream of the bay. Then, tying it to some low bushes near some knee-high grass, he loosened the cinch strap. Taking the package Joan had provided from the saddle bag, he noted the letter she had given him for Martin.

The package contained two slices of buttered bread and a thick slice of cheese. While he ate the meal, Oli noticed that the paper it was wrapped in was the tally list the merchant had made. He reviewed the list: Beans, coffee, salt, cold flour, a side of bacon, and some items that could be used for cuts or wounds.

His thoughts went back to the ledger he had carried on the last trip. His father had taught him that if you write down your assets, you then know what is necessary to go forward. This trip was shorter, so he did not think it was necessary to keep such close track.

Back on the bay, he rode through rolling hills, passing an occasional homestead. A large dog rushed toward them from one farm, stopping short of the road. Oli tapped the bay's flanks, urging it to move faster, putting distance between the dog and them.

Thanks to the number of people traveling west, there were well-marked roads to travel. An occasional town would provide a place to purchase additional supplies as necessary. He chose to sleep under the stars the first night. With the sun low in the western sky, he stopped along the banks of a river.

The fire was crackling and a pot of water for coffee was sitting next to the flames before he took care of the bay. Stripping the saddle from the horse and putting a halter in place of the bit and reins, he picketed the horse on a nearby patch of grass. Taking handfuls of grass, he gave it a good rubdown.

Returning to the fire, the water was boiling. He measured coffee into the water. Slicing some bacon into a pan, he enjoyed the smell of the meat. The horse had made good time today. It had been a long day. Oli thought back to the horse he'd gone west with on the earlier trip. He had called it the *good horse*. It was old and had a bad leg. It was all he had been able to afford at the time. It could not compare to the strength and stamina of the bay. But he had never known a horse that was a better friend, or had more heart.

With his evening meal finished and the dishes taken care of, Oli checked on the bay. It was standing with its head up, listening to something on their back trail. It was possibly another traveler or a wild animal. He trusted the bay's senses and watched the trail for a while before bedding down with the Paterson under his saddle and the Hawken under the edge of his blanket. Settling his head against the saddle, he tipped his hat down over his face and drifted off into blissful sleep.

The sun was up when Oli opened his eyes. For a moment he was confused about where he was. Sitting up quickly, realization came that he had slept too soundly and too long. Habits like that could be very risky as he traveled west. Drinking the cold coffee from the night before and quickly breaking camp, he saddled the bay and headed out. As he entered the road, he caught the smell of tobacco smoke. The bay was eager to go, so he let it have its head for the first few miles.

Oli realized he had the same fear he'd thought was overcome years ago. Maybe it was the possibility of being followed, or maybe the realization that he was alone on the road. He decided to spend the next night or two in a convenient town. By that time his senses should sharpen and he would be ready to face the dangers of the wide-open spaces.

Riding steadily with just a short rest in the early afternoon, Oli reached a small settlement on the Cedar River named Prairie Rapids Crossing. One of the residents had a small hotel. Riding up to the hitching post, he tied the tired bay and stiffly walked into the entrance. The lobby contained a couple of worn chairs. A gray haired man slouched behind the counter, reading a local paper. Looking up, he appraised his guest.

"Lookin fur a room, or supper?" the man asked.

"Both, if you can," replied Oli. "Also need a place for my horse."

"Got money?" the clerk grunted. "A dollar fur the room. Half-dollar fur supper and breakfast, and another half-dollar fur your horse. Got a shed out back fur the horse. Includes some oats and hay."

"Sounds good. I'll take care of my horse first."

"Cash first, mister," the clerk said.

After settling up with the clerk, Oli led his horse around back. His clothing was dusty and disheveled from travel. It may have set the clerk to wondering if he had money for the room. He found the shed for the horse, or the excuse for a shed. Several boards were missing and it leaned to the left. The door hung loose on leather hinges. It could not be closed due to slanting of the door jams. There was a decent stall and hay available. The oats were mostly grass seeds, but the horse seemed to like them. After giving the bay a proper rubdown and some water, he headed for the hotel, carrying his saddlebags and Hawken.

Alongside the shed was a lean-to that served as a toilet. The stench brought his attention to it. Taking a moment, Oli relieved himself, admitting that once he got past the odor, it beat squatting in the bushes.

The hotel was a single-story frame building consisting of the lobby, a small dining room, and a narrow hall with four curtained doorways. Oli had been directed to the second room. Pushing the curtain aside, he saw a single, narrow bunk to one side. Next to it was a small stand with a bowl containing a pitcher filled with water for washing up.

The room had no window, so Oli left the curtain on the door open to allow feeble light into the room. After shoving the saddlebags and Hawken under the bunk, Oli poured some water in the bowl and washed the dust off his face and hands. A threadbare towel hung from a peg on the side of the stand to dry with.

Pulling the curtain closed, Oli headed for the dining room. He hadn't eaten much and his stomach was aching with hunger. The dining room was just off a small kitchen and consisted of one long table with eight chairs. Oli chose a seat that would allow him to see out the fly-specked window.

The clerk and his wife owned the hotel. She did the cooking. What it lacked in taste was made up for in quantity. A large pot of beans and hard bread made up the dinner. A dish of salted fat served as butter for the bread. Oli and one other man were the only diners. He appeared to be a drummer who ate heartily.

He talked of life on the road and the items he sold for the eastern warehouse. Eating sparingly of the beans and dipping the hard bread into the juice, Oli half-listened to the man. The drummer spoke of his next stop at the juncture of the Raccoon and Des Moines Rivers. It was a recently abandoned fort about four days' travel away. Suddenly, he had Oli's attention.

"A fort about four days away?" Oli asked.

The question seemed to surprise the drummer. Evidently, he accepted the fact that people didn't listen to him and wasn't expecting a response. "Yes sir, it's a fine place to stop. They call it Fort Des Moines. The army left it earlier this year. Local folks took it over."

"Mind if we travel together?" Oli inquired.

The portly drummer smiled from ear to ear. "Not at all, my friend. Nice to have company on the road. By the way, the name's Sal Rawlins."

Awkwardly, Sal reached a hand across the table. Accepting it, Oli replied, "I'm Oli August of Elkader. I am headed for Fort Leavenworth."

"I will be headed that way myself after a couple of other stops," Sal said.

The prospect of having company on the road opened a floodgate of conversation from the drummer. It was another hour and the sun had set before Oli was able to graciously excuse himself.

Stopping for a moment in the lobby, he heard an out of tune piano playing in a dimly lit building across the street. Crossing the muddy street, he stepped in, taking a moment for his eyes to adjust. There was a plank bar running along the right side and a greasy haired man tending customers. A skinny man in a stained white shirt pounded out tunes on the piano.

A few tables with stools filled the rest of the saloon. At one of the tables, four men were playing cards. Two middle-aged women in brightly colored dresses moved around the room. A lone man leaned on the bar at the back. He looked up quickly when Oli walked in and then turned his back to the door.

Stepping up to the bar, the bartender came over and asked him what he would like. "I'll have rye," Oli responded.

Setting a glass down, the bartender asked, "You want the bottle?"

"Nope, just a drink."

Picking up the glass with the amber liquid, Oli took a sip. As he did so, the man at the end of the bar walked out behind him. He got a glimpse of the man's face in the dirty mirror on the wall behind the bar. It looked familiar, but he couldn't place it. He turned to take a second look as the man disappeared out the door.

The rye was okay. When offered, he let the bartender pour a second shot. The rye warmed his stomach and made his head a bit light. He smelled the heavy scent of the lady before he saw her moving up next to him. He could feel her heat through the bright dress and smelled her sweat coming through the perfume.

"Buy a girl a drink?" she asked. "Maybe a couple and we can get to know each other better."

On cue, the bartender was in front of them with an uncorked bottle of rye. He smiled and tilted the bottle toward Oli.

"Pour the lady one, but none for me," he said, dropping a coin onto the bar and heading for the door. The cool night air smelled refreshing. Heading across to the hotel, Oli caught the glow of someone smoking in the shadows up the street. Frowning, he entered the hotel and picked up a lit candle in the lobby, then headed for the room. Was someone following him? If so, why? The prospect of having the drummer with him for the next few days was looking better all the time.

After placing the candle onto the small stand, Oli checked under the bunk. It appeared that his gear was as he'd left it. He then sat on the bunk to remove his boots, the hay tick mattress sagging down due to its loose strapping. Laughing, Oli muttered, "I guess it beats sleeping on the ground, but not by much."

The clerk's wife had breakfast ready just as the

sun peeked over the eastern horizon. The uncomfortable bed made sure that the blond man hadn't overslept. Oli met the drummer in the small dining room. His face fell as the owner's wife emerged from the kitchen with the same large pot of beans. They were steaming hot and a little thicker than the night before. On her second trip she brought out a pan of biscuits and a bowl of honey.

While the drummer shoved large spoonfuls of beans into his mouth, Oli took several biscuits and poured honey over them. A pot of brisk coffee proved to be the best part of the meal. Honey was added to the brew and was a perfect companion for the slightly dry and tough biscuits.

With breakfast over, the drummer headed for the rickety outhouse. "I'll be right back," he called over his shoulder. "Already got my horses out front."

Oli was surprised to see that two horses were tied to the rail in front of the hotel, one with a saddle, the other with a pack. He hurried to the shed to get the bay and was treated to the grunts and groans from inside the outhouse.

With the bay saddled and the Hawken in the scabbard, Oli led the animal to a watering trough. Sal came through the hotel carrying a carpet bag with his personal belongings. Oli complimented the man, "You have good-looking stock. I noticed you didn't keep them in the back."

Grinning, Sal replied, "I save a dollar and put them up at my customer's barn."

The road out of Prairie Rapids Crossing followed the Cedar River. Oli led the way, with the drummer and his pack animal close behind. They were barely in the saddle when Sal started telling stories of life on the road. Each story took about 10 minutes and always seemed to remind him of another. Some of the stories supplied useful information about best routes, good camping areas, and warnings about less than ethical hotels or saloons. Much of it was about looking for the big sale.

About two hours out of town, Sal hollered for Oli to wait a minute. Looking back, he saw the drummer disappearing into the bushes. Once again the chorus of grunts was heard. Smiling, Oli thought, *Too many beans, my friend.*

Near mid-afternoon they saw that the road split away from the river. The cedar trees and other brush disappeared behind the rolling plains. Spring flowers were in full bloom with splashes of yellow, red, and blue. During a brief stop for rest, Oli found a patch of wild strawberries. A few extra minutes were taken while he and Sal ate their fill.

A couple hours before dark, Oli asked the drummer to continue riding for another hour. Watching Sal ride on without question, the blond-haired man rode to the top of a rise just south of them. It would give Oli a good view of their back trail. He could not shake the feeling that someone was following them.

Then again, he knew it could just be another traveler with the same destination. They had kept up a constant pace and the person behind might not have had a chance to catch up. The rise ran for some distance on the south side of the road. From the top, Oli could see a couple of miles in each direction. The two-track road wound back behind them, disappearing into the depressions of the plain.

After watching for an hour and not seeing any movement, he rode along the top of the hill, trying to stay over the edge so as not to skyline himself. Just before dark he saw smoke from beyond a rise. His guess was that it would be Sal.

Suddenly, the bay shied away from something. It was a large jackrabbit. Drawing the Paterson from his holster, Oli leveled the gun and fired. The rabbit rolled over, kicking its last. The bay jumped slightly from the sound of the revolver, but quickly quieted with some gentle pats on the side of its neck.

Riding up to the camp, he found Sal busy heating water in a Dutch oven and adding coffee to a boiling pot. Oli was impressed with the location and the tidy camp that was set up. The drummer knew how to live on the road.

"Heard your shot," Sal said. "I figured it had to be a bird or rabbit. Got a pot of water warming for a hearty soup."

"I'll clean the rabbit before putting up the bay," Oli offered.

While dressing the rabbit he saw the drummer bring a couple of potatoes, wild onions, and a turnip from the pack. Handing the skinned rabbit to Sal, Oli decided to ride up to the rise for one more look around. The sun had set and any fire could be seen for a distance. That is, unless the follower was clever enough to keep to low ground.

After watching the back trail for 20 minutes, Oli turned the bay back toward their camp. Stopping abruptly, he stood in the stirrups, looking up the road head. He caught the flicker of firelight in a cluster of trees about a mile ahead.

Sal had the stew boiling and was just mixing in some cornmeal flour when Oli returned. Loosening the cinch on the bay, he tied it to some low brush.

"After eating, I need to check on something ahead of us," he informed Sal.

"Shouldn't be over 10 more minutes. I got us some biscuits from the hotel. She knows I like to eat and usually gives me a bunch to take with me," Sal said proudly as he tested a piece of potato.

"There was this one trip that I had to move at night . . ." he began with another story.

Half listening, Oli wondered about the traveler in front of them. Sal made quite a display setting up the meal. After commenting on the hearty meal, he fell silent, his thoughts elsewhere. Normally a traveler would join up with others on the road for companionship and to share a meal. Whoever was in front of them didn't want company.

With the meal done, Sal offered to clean up while Oli checked out the fire ahead of them. The bay took some urging to move away from the camp. It was ready to have the saddle off and get a good roll in the thick plains grass.

Oli moved to high country as he rode ahead. The moon was in the first quarter and just coming over the horizon. The yelps of fox and a chorus of crickets filled the damp night air. The bay's steps were muffled by the thick grass.

He smelled smoke before he reached the camp. It came from a smoldering fire. Whoever was ahead of them must have let the fire die after supper. Leaving the bay tied to a sapling, he continued ahead on foot, the Hawken cradled in his arm.

Coming over the rise short of the camp, Oli searched the dark camp for its occupants. A few coals glowed red in the fire, occasionally snapping into a brief flame. Slowly moving forward, he took care not to step on any dry twigs, giving his approach away. Just short of the camp, he crouched in some blackberry brambles. He did not dare move for fear that thorns would drag against his clothing.

After several minutes, Oli concluded that the person who had eaten here had left. His guess was that the person was sleeping away from the fire to prevent being found. The cold realization swept over him that it was possible that the individual had moved back toward their camp. They may have passed in the night, unaware of each other. Worse yet, he may have been spotted by the other and could be stalked even now.

Deciding to come back and check the camp out more the next morning, he moved out of the brambles. They scratched at his face and hands and penetrated his clothing as he moved back toward the bay. Oli stopped just short and watched the bay in the low moonlight. It was calmly pulling at the sapling leaves.

Fighting the desire to gallop back to their camp, he forced himself to keep the bay at a walk. He watched for movement before coming into the camp. There was none. Maybe Sal had decided to turn in before he got back. Stopping just outside the firelight, Oli realized that something was wrong. Sal's horses were gone!

Moving around the perimeter, he saw that the drummer's packs had been gone through and items lay strewn around. He could see Sal's bedroll neatly laid out with the saddle still at the end, awaiting the owner's tired head.

Fear clutched Oli's stomach. There was a good chance that Sal may have been killed by the intruder. If there had been a shot, odds are he would have heard it. Tying the bay, he began to circle out from the camp, looking to see if he could find the drummer's body. He also realized that whoever did this could be hiding in the dark, waiting for him to come back.

He smelled Sal before he saw him. Lying near some brush was the drummer. His pants were down around his knees and he lay on his side. In the low light, it appeared that there was something dark on the side of his balding head.

Taking care not to step in Sal's business, Oli knelt to check for a pulse. As he reached and felt the neck, the drummer groaned. Startled by the sound, he jumped back, soiling his boot heel.

"Damn you, Sal! You are as bad as a goose. You shove it in one end and out it comes out from the other," he complained.

Carefully rolling the man clear of the bush, he pulled up the pants and then carried him to the bedroll. While he was doing this, there was a tingle along his spine as he expected to be attacked from behind at anytime. Seeing the bay standing with its head hanging gave him some comfort that they were alone.

Adding wood to the fire, Oli got some water heating. Returning to the drummer, he could see the ugly gash on his head. He carefully cleaned around it with a damp rag. Groaning again, Sal opened his eyes.

"What the hell happened?" he asked. "I go out

to take an evening constitution and lights explode in my head." "Oh," he closed his eyes from the pain. "Damn, it hurts."

"Stay still, Sal," he cautioned him. "You could have a cracked skull. I need to take care of my horse and I'll be right back to finish cleaning and bandaging your head."

He could hear the drummer complaining near the fire while he took care of the bay. Stripping the saddle and bridle, he picketed it closer than the stolen horses had been.

"You had a hard day, boy," he said, scratching the side of the bay's head. "I've a feeling you will get some rest tomorrow."

The bay whinnied softly, responding to its owner's voice. He promised to come back and give the bay a good rubdown after taking care of Sal's head wound.

It turned out that Sal hadn't seen anything. He'd been hit from behind while in a compromising position. He had nothing of real value. There were only a few trinkets and catalogs to give to customers. He carried only enough food to get from town to town. His money belt was still intact around his waist.

Oli sat pondering the night's events while sipping on some stale coffee left over from supper. After brushing the bay, he moved it near their blankets. It would give them an alarm in case of an intruder.

The position of the stars told him that it was after midnight. He could hear the even breathing of Sal. Oli lay awake thinking about the theft. Other than the horses, it did not appear that anything else had been taken. It had just been scattered. Maybe it was supposed to look like a robbery. His brow furled as Oli wondered, *Could it be someone wanted to prevent Sal from riding with me?*

What advantage would there be by him traveling alone? Oli knew that by himself he would be traveling faster and be harder to follow. Could it be that someone wanted him alone to get rid of him without witnesses? It was not that unusual for a lone traveler to disappear without explanation.

Long after he'd climbed into his blankets, his mind kept working on theories. Somewhere along the line, he fell into restless sleep.

CHAPTER THREE

Daylight found Oli sitting next to a small fire, sipping coffee and eating a couple of stale biscuits. He could hear Sal's heavy breathing and occasional groan. He had changed the dressing on the head wound. It was a horrible blue gash, no doubt from the barrel of a gun. The left eye had swollen to a slit and it would be a while before the drummer would be able to see out of it.

With enough light to try and put together what might have happened, Oli tossed the dregs out of his cup. After checking on Sal, he began to look for tracks. The intruder's boot prints were plain to see as he had moved around the camp scattering items. He found additional tracks leaving the camp along the road.

The man had gone back into the trees about 100 paces up the road. This was where the man had tied his horse beneath a spreading oak. On a hunch, Oli climbed into the lower branches of the oak. He was able to see their camp from the perch.

Climbing back down, Oli noticed the butt of a slim cigar with a well chewed end near the trunk. He had seen something similar for sale in the mercantile in Elkader. Soldiers returning from the Mexican war liked smoking the slim, dark tobacco cigars called cigarros. If the man had smoked it while watching, he would have kept the glowing end shielded and the breeze from the north would have carried any smell away.

He also noticed that the attacker's horse had been tied to the tree for some time by the amount of droppings. Oli thought about the night before, realizing that he and Sal hadn't taken precautions to keep their eyes on their surroundings, or even away from the cook fire, risking night blindness.

The night before, Oli had thought he'd located the other traveler and had assumed the man had settled down in front of them. He had also underestimated the viciousness of the man traveling near them. He vowed that these mistakes would not be repeated.

It appeared that the man had watched them until Sal was alone. Then, when the opportunity presented itself, he had moved in and attacked Sal. After spreading the packs around, he'd gone back to the oak, leading Sal's stock.

Oli saddled the bay and picked up the trail of the attacker. The man had gone up the rise and circled wide of the decoy camp. It appeared that the attacker was leaving the area. After a couple of miles, Oli turned back, not wanting to leave Sal alone too long. He found the drummer sitting up, drinking lukewarm coffee.

"I feel like a buffalo herd run over me," he said,

looking up at Oli.

"We were outsmarted by the hombre," Oli admitted.

"He took my horses didn't he?"

"The horses are the only things taken. The pack was emptied but the items were left." Rubbing his chin, Oli continued, "I believe his goal was to slow us down or make sure you couldn't keep traveling with me."

"Are you sure?" Sal asked. "I had some good horses. Maybe he was just after horseflesh and couldn't care less about the two of us."

"That might be so," Oli replied. "The trouble is, someone was following me before we met."

"If he wanted to get at you, why would he bother giving me a lump on the head?" Sal asked. "He could have just taken you while you were scouting away from our camp."

"I agree it doesn't make much sense." Turning to Sal, he continued. "First, I will find a place where you can mend. Then, I will find the man that did this. If he has your horses, I will leave them at Fort Des Moines at a livery stable."

Satisfied to sit and watch Oli as he collected the scattered items back into the packs, Sal remained put and complained about his bad luck and how it could affect his sales. With only one horse and all of the gear, Oli knew that he was going to lose time on the way to Leavenworth.

With Sal and his belongings on the bay, Oli walked carrying his own saddlebags and the Hawken. There was sign of the attacker and the stolen horses on the road. Evidently the thief was confident that the two men wouldn't be able to catch up. It was two days before they came upon a small cluster of buildings. The man who had stolen the horses had left the road before reaching the small town. One of the buildings had "Groceries" painted across it.

Leading the bay and its cargo, to the sagging hitching rail, Oli tied the horse and hung his saddle bags over the rail. After helping Sal down, the two of them entered the grocer's. A man in a crisp white shirt and brown apron sat on a stool at the end of the counter.

He looked up and smiled at the two potential customers, "Welcome to Willow. We're a small but friendly little town. I carry about everything a traveling man might need, including whiskey."

"First off, we need a doctor for my friend here," Oli replied.

Having his first good look at Sal's swollen eye and bandaged head, the grocer gasped, "Damnit man! Were you kicked by a mule?"

"Not a mule," Oli informed him. "A lowlife blindsided him using the barrel of his revolver."

"We ain't got us a doc, but Hanson at the smithy got a little training in the army," the grocer said.

The smithy wasn't much more than an open lean-to with an anvil and forge. The lean-to was attached to a single-room structure that served as his home. The lean, scarred blacksmith was shoeing a horse when they walked up. Sal was getting around a little better, but his normal gab was missing.

Between the blacksmith and the grocer, Oli's

problems with Sal were quickly cleared up. The drummer would be able to stay with the smithy and the grocer said a freight wagon would be coming through in the next couple of weeks and Sal could hitch a ride to Fort Des Moines.

Oli picked up a few items at the grocer before leaving without spending a night. He had already lost too much time. While he was walking, Oli had estimated that the thief was staying about a half-day ahead of them. While the man had ridden wide of the small town, Oli expected to pick it up again beyond it.

The trail was picked up a few miles beyond the town, only this time the tracks were fresher. There was sign of a place along the road where the man had waited. Dismounting to look the place over, Oli found several cigarro butts. Looking toward the town, Oli realized that the man could see anyone riding in this direction. The road followed the river, making this destination much longer than line of sight.

He suddenly realized that he was being led! Led for what purpose, he did not know. The man was controlling the destination. Oli knew he shouldn't take time to try and catch the man. Getting to Fort Leavenworth and seeing Martin was the key objective. But with all that had happened the past few days, he would have to invest the time to discover who the man was and stop him.

Oli knew that he was not a hunter of men. His skills had been learned the hard way, while he'd been lost in the wilderness searching for gold. He prayed that they would be sufficient against whoever was out there. It was time to review his assets to accomplish the upcoming task.

His skill with a rifle was better than average. With the knife he was very good, but with his revolver, he had to take time and then was not confident of hitting what he shot at. The rabbit he had shot a few days earlier had been as much luck as skill.

Oli had learned tracking and stealth in the woods. If necessary, he could live off the land for weeks at a time. He could make fire with sticks if no other means were available. After having to live on raw meat when traveling the wild country nine years ago, learning to make fire had been a priority. He could make tools and weapons out of trees or stones. Oli had long had the skill to craft wood.

Sitting on the bay, he surveyed that area. One thing he was sure of was that the attacker was watching him. While he could not see the man, he could feel the eyes upon him. To the north, he knew there was marsh along the Iowa River. He had hunted waterfowl there four years ago. He was a day's ride from the river. Turning the bay north, he took off at a trot.

In a matter of hours the terrain changed from rolling plains to small streams lined with willow and cottonwood. Oli took advantage of the streams, riding in the water to make tracking him a bit more difficult, therefore delaying the follower. But he made sure that the exits from the water were in sandy or clay-covered areas so the man would not completely lose the trail.

When leaving the water on a wide, sandy strip, he stopped for a quick meal. He made a small fire next to the water using dry, fast-burning willow branches. His goal was to give the man the impression that he wasn't worried about being followed.

The sun was low in the western sky when Oli

31

reached the marshes. His stomach was aching with hunger. The jerky eaten earlier had stopped satisfying. The bay was tired and slowing. It was time to find out who was behind him. He swung down from the horse. Digging a portion of oats from the saddle bags for the animal and a piece of jerky for himself, the two stood among the cattails, hearing the calls and splashes of ducks and geese, as they returned to the water after feeding on the plains.

As he stepped out, leading the horse, Oli felt calmness wash over him. He was in his element, and was now on offence. With the sound of the bullfrogs, honking of the geese, and the chorus of peepers surrounding him, he pushed through tall swamp grass and around clumps of dense cedars. He could hear the sucking sounds as the bay pulled its hooves out of the soft, water-logged ground.

He was heading back to the south. About an hour back there had been a hogback that would give a good view of the swampy valley. The man he was hunting might be using the very narrow ridge to watch for Oli's fire. After reaching the more solid ground along the edge of the swamp, he mounted the bay and continued heading for the high ground.

The moon was just breaking the horizon when the base of the hogback was reached. Oli moved into some tree cover and stripped the saddle from the bay. Giving it a quick rubdown with cedar boughs, he picketed it near an area to graze while keeping it in the shadows of the trees.

Looking up the steep side of the hill, the top could be identified by the cutoff of the night stars. Moving like a ghost in the night, he carefully worked his way up the hillside. There was no need to hurry and take a chance of making noise. The man he was searching for would be camped for the night.

Reaching the top, he gazed at the moonlit valley below. The soft night breeze brought the pungent smells of the swamp. Sitting quietly in the dark, he listened for any sounds that did not fit into the nightlife. The crest of the narrow ridge ran northeast and southwest. It was lower toward the northeast, eventually ending at the Iowa River bank.

He had ridden around the end near the river. If the man had stopped on the hill to watch, he should be between this location and the river. After a moment's rest, Oli continued to move along the ridge, taking advantage of a game trail. Less than 20 minutes later, he caught the smell of tobacco smoke. Silently, he sank into the deeper shadows.

He knew that the smell of smoke could be picked up from some distance when carried by a soft breeze. Carefully, he checked his Hawken rifle to make sure it hadn't become fouled during the night stalking. A quick check of the revolver and the Good Knife left him confident that he was ready to meet whomever it was out there in the dark.

Moving a few feet at a time and then listening, he crept slowly along the ridge. Long stretches were void of trees or brush for cover. By staying below the top, Oli was able to keep to the deeper shadows not penetrated by the rising moon. Again he smelled the smoke. It was stronger now.

Oli's heart began to pound in his chest. The man he was looking for could be just a stone's throw away. He was located above him, based on the soft night breeze.

A slow search along the hillside revealed an area of dense shadows made up of either rocks or brush. Below him, toward the swamp, the frogs and geese continued to fill the night air with their calls. In the distance, coyotes howled as they hunted for prey. In silence, Oli searched the dark mass, planning his next move.

He almost jumped out of his skin when he heard the snort of horses just below him. An animal or something had moved near them, causing the challenge. The damp night air and the unexpected sound made him shiver, as he realized how close he was to the man. The sound of cloth against rock brought his attention back to the shadows. The man had moved, maybe glancing toward the horses, or possibly trying to get a better view of the valley.

After 10 minutes of lying motionless, Oli's muscles began to ache. Even with the cool night air, he could feel the sweat running down his back under the woolen shirt. There was a cough and the sound of someone repositioning them self. The dark mass was even closer than first estimated. Any sound would alert the man to his presence.

At last, a cloud drifted over the moon, plunging the landscape into obscurity. Without hesitation, Oli moved up the hillside, taking every precaution not to make noise. Once on the summit, he laid in some low brush and waited for the moon to reappear. Oli froze. Not 20 feet away, the outline of the man materialized among some stunted trees.

He could feel his legs trembling along with the pounding of his heart. The Hawken lay near his side, aimed in the direction of the man. If he tried to raise it, the moonlight on the barrel would give him away. It was time to make a move. Taking a deep breath to try and quiet his nerves, he spoke softly.

"I have you covered, mister, don't move."

In a quick, fluid movement the man spun and drew his sidearm. The flash of the weapon was blinding. Oli felt something tug at this boot heel as he rolled away, barely getting out of the path of the next shot. Again on his stomach, the Hawken was in position to fire and he squeezed off a shot in the man's direction.

Unable to pick a target out in the darkness because of the muzzle flash, he continued to roll over the edge of the ridge. Sliding down the hillside several feet, he came up against a rotting windfall. Oli lay motionless, searching the ridge above him for the man. His left leg was twisted beneath him and burned with pain. Finding it impossible to bear, he pulled himself along the hill just enough to take the weight off his leg.

He heard the man running. He was headed for the horses! Leaping to his feet, Oli took a step and went down again when his foot twisted under him. Something was stuck to his boot. Reaching down, he realized that the heel had been torn mostly off by the man's shot.

Pulling off the boot, he continued up the hill with his rifle in one hand and the boot in the other. There was no way he was leaving the boot behind and ending up barefoot. Scrambling up the hill and over the summit, he had just started down when the sounds of a running horse reached him. Sinking into a sitting position, he gasped for air. The pounding of his heart and his own breathing made it impossible to hear the direction that the horse had taken.

Abruptly, he realized for the moment that he was safe. The man was running and he was still the hunter. Catching his breath, he began to take stock. The heel was mostly intact. The bullet had pulled the nails loose and it hung to the side, causing him to trip earlier. This could be fixed. He still had the Hawken, his revolver, and the Good Knife.

Tonight, he had underestimated the quickness and willingness of his prey to kill, a mistake he would not make again. Using the butt of the revolver, he secured the heel on the boot. A quick fix, but it should work until he got to another town.

Heading down the hill, he found where the man had kept the horses. Oli was pleased to find that he had only taken his own horse. Sal's horses were still on their pickets. The friendly whinnies of the animals were comforting.

Leading the horses back to where he had left the bay, Oli spread out his blankets and laid down for a couple hours of sleep. He was exhausted and was depending on the bay to warn him of anyone trying to get close. Tossing and turning restlessly, he dreamed about an animal with hot breath chasing him. He opened his eyes and was face-to-face with one of Sal's horses.

Startled, he rolled away before realizing what it was. Equally surprised by the sudden movement, the horse trotted away to the other animals. Evidently, the picket rope had come loose.

Light was just beginning to show in the sky above the hogback. It was time to get up. Slowly sitting up in his long johns and stocking feet, Oli looked around for any signs of danger. The man he was hunting might be coming back to locate him, but he doubted it would be before daylight. By the sounds of the running horse the night before, he was putting distance between them.

Building a small fire to make coffee, he remembered that all he'd eaten the day before had been jerky. His stomach was begging for food. He put a second pot next to the fire to heat some water for breakfast. Once the water was hot, he would mix some cold flour in and make a kind of gruel. It would be nice and filling.

Returning from taking care of the horses and his morning constitution, he found the coffee water boiling and the pot of water steaming. In a few minutes, he was sitting down to coffee and hot mush. As he ate, he watched and listened to the cedar thicket around him. It was unlikely anyone could sneak up on him here.

With the bay saddled and the other horses in tow, he headed back to the spot the man had ridden away from. He dismounted a hundred paces away and led the horses. Just short of the spot, he tied the animals and continued on foot. A quick circle around the area revealed the direction in which the man had ridden. Turning back to get his horses, Oli stopped suddenly. On the leaves there were some drops of blood! He had wounded the man.

Following the tracks back to where the man had kept the horses, he found several more splatters of blood. He knew that this might change the stakes of this hunt. While the man might be even more dangerous once he was caught up with, his desire to find Oli would be far less.

The bay nickered softly as he approached the horses. Swinging up into the saddle, he continued to follow the departing man's trail. He realized that while finding Sal's horses was a good thing, but having them in tow was making tracking the man harder.

The man had galloped only a short distance before slowing the horse to a walk. He must have been tired of the cedar branches slapping his face. He found a spot where the man had stopped to bandage his wound. As best Oli could figure, by the height of the blood on the cedars, it was a low wound.

The man had continued to ride toward the swamp. There was a possibility that he could double back and lie in wait to ambush him. By the time Oli was a half-mile from the swamp, the concern was strong enough that he rode wide of the man's trail in the same general direction. Just shy of the swamp, he watered the horses in a small pool. Tying them loosely to some willow branches, he continued on foot. If something happened to him, the animals would eventually pull the ropes loose and wander away after water and food.

Cutting back across the front of the swamp, he found the man's trail. Less than a quarter-mile into the swamp, he spotted the man's horse beyond some cattails, standing and chewing on some edible shoots. A closer look showed that it was dragging the reins and there was a dark stain on the saddle.

As he watched the horse, he heard someone cough. Moving cautiously, he crept in the direction of the noise. Lying against a willow tree was the man.

The lower front of his shirt and trousers were covered with blood. His revolver lay on the ground beside him. Oli lined the man up in the sights of the Hawken.

"You move this time, and I will blow you wide open," he warned.

Looking up, the wounded man replied in a weak voice, "I am done in. You got me bad."

Again, he coughed and winced with pain.

"Toss the gun away," Oli ordered.

With a shaky hand, the man pushed the revolver further from his side. As though it had been a great effort, his chin then dropped to his chest.

Oli slowly moved up to the man's side and kicked the gun well out of reach. He looked to see if there were any other weapons. He opened the shirt and looked at the wound. It was blue-gray and swollen. The bullet had gone in the lower front and exited a bit higher in the back. A lot of blood had been lost.

He could not just leave the man where he lay. Putting a pile of dry sticks together, soon there was a pot of water warming to clean the wound.

"My name is Wilber Hill. They call me Will. I got some cigarros in my shirt. Can you light one for me?"

Taking a slim cigar, Oli lit it with a burning ember from the fire. The dark, rich tobacco burned the tissues of his mouth. Kneeling next to Will, he put the cigar in his lips. He then moved back to the fire and dipped a neckerchief in the hot water.

Carefully, he cleaned the wound and applied a bandage made from strips torn from a spare shirt. He then planned to make a broth and look for some plants to make a poultice that would help prevent infection.

Leaning over the fire and adding bits of jerky to the pot to make a broth, he heard the man groan as he moved to sit up a bit more.

"You best lay still. You don't want to start the bleeding again," he warned.

"I got a couple things I got to say." Will's voice sounded stronger. "I'm sorry about what I done to the man you was traveling with. I was paid to follow you and didn't want him being with you to slow your travel."

"Who would pay you to follow me?"

Ignoring Oli's question, Will continued. "Once you got to Fort Leavenworth, my job was done. I wanted to head for Texas. Got a deal down there to make some quick money."

He began to cough again, dropping the cigar as he grabbed his midsection. Blood began to weep through the bandages. Oli moved over to the man and helped him lay back down. He put the smoldering tobacco out with the toe of his boot.

Slowly, he opened his pain-filled eyes. "Don't let me die. I didn't mean to shoot at you. I was surprised and couldn't help reacting."

"I will do what I can. After taking care of the horses, I will put a poultice together. Just lay there. I'll hurry back."

Oli stripped the saddles and picketed the horses on some grass. He then found the leaves he wanted. While he crushed them in some warm water, he could hear the wounded man's heavy breathing.

Will was unconscious when he changed the

bandage and applied the hot mixture. He looked at the deathly pale face and said a quick prayer for the man.

Supper was a simple meal. He drank coffee and fried some salt pork. He soaked some hard bread in the grease. He drank a little of the broth. The rest he saved for Will when he woke back up.

Sitting away from the fire, Oli sipped coffee, smoothing his moustache between drinks. Night had come to the swamp and the nightlife came alive. Mosquitoes searched out any exposed skin to drink their fill of blood. Frogs and night birds filled the darkness with sounds. The air was heavy with the smell of rotting swamp vegetation. He knew he had to continue on to Fort Leavenworth to visit Martin. He knew that he owed this man nothing. Yet Will couldn't be moved and Oli's conscience wouldn't let him abandon him.

Crushing a mosquito that landed on his cheek, he wished Will had drank some of the broth. A chilling breeze started over the swamp. It would help with the biting insects.

In the dark, Will cleared his throat. "Can you hear me?" he asked.

"Yes, yes I can. I have some broth for you to drink."

"Why would Jacob Wolfe want to know if you got to . . . Leavenworth?" his weak voice inquired.

So it was Jacob, Oli thought. Stopping by the fire, he poured some broth into a cup. Moving to Will's side, he answered, "It might be an issue of Spanish gold. I had some when I first got to town and he has always thought there was more."

Looking down at the ashen face of the man in the glow of the small fire, he stopped short. Will lay there looking into the night with unseeing eyes. Oli sat back, his legs too weak to hold him. He had shot and killed this man. He now had the life of another man to answer for at the gates of heaven.

He placed his hand on the chest of the man, hoping to feel some sign of life. He sat for a long moment praying for the departed man's soul. He then knew he had to leave this spot. Not in the morning, but tonight.

A shallow grave was hastily dug, using the frying pan. He dragged Will's lifeless body, wrapped in a blanket, and rolled it into the depression. Filling the grave and piling all available rocks onto the mound, he put out the fire and collected his and Will's items. Keeping the North Star over his right shoulder, he left the swamp riding the bay and leading three horses.

The rising sun found him back on the trail to Des Moines. He was traveling fast, switching his saddle from one horse to another. The plan was to leave Sal's horses there and take Will's along to Fort Leavenworth. He had lost too much time with the tragic cat and mouse game played the past few days.

While sitting under a cottonwood for his midday meal, he went through the items he had taken from Will's pockets and the stuff from his saddle bags. They contained little more than what is normally found on a man who lived on the move. There was a clipping from a newspaper describing a gun for hire who fit Will's description. There were five eagle gold pieces and a small amount of other money. There was also a letter from a sister in Virginia.

Once he got to Des Moines, Oli planned to sell the man's belongings and send the money with a note to the sister. He hoped he could come up with what he needed to say in the note before arriving.

The town was located at the juncture of the Des Moines and Raccoon Rivers. It was built around an abandoned fort. The town was poorly laid out, with old and new construction of buildings using various materials. It was surrounded by rolling plains. His first stop was at a livery to leave Sal's horses.

The stay was short in Des Moines and the note, lacking in specifics, was sent. At least Will wouldn't be one of those lost without any word getting back to their families. He let the sister know the grave was prayed over and death had come quickly. If the sister knew how her brother made his living, she could conclude what had killed him. After the sale of Will's horse and his guns, there was just over $100 included with the note. Little enough after a man's lifetime.

It felt good to be back on the road, heading for his objective. It would be about 4-5 days' ride to Fort Leavenworth. Oli had sent word back to Joan, assuring her that he was well, and of the expected arrival date at the fort. With the burden of the extra horses and carrying information about a dead man off his shoulders, he could now concentrate on the task ahead: Finding out if he could help Martin.

The best route out of Des Moines was along the Raccoon River Valley. The valley had cottonwood and oak trees lining the banks. The beauty of the valley and open plains rising on each side was exhilarating. The purple petals of the jack-in-the-pulpit and white flowers of the bloodroot filled the valley, while yellow tickseed and dark pink prairie smoke covered the plains. Spring and early summer were a celebration of life on the Great Plains.

After a half-day's ride, Oli turned south along a well-marked road towards Fort Leavenworth. The ordeal of the past few days was soon pushed to the back of his mind. It was replaced by the excitement of seeing new country. It brought back memories of the trip he had made west with Jack Albert's wagon train in 1839.

The bay was in good condition, despite the fast travel after the burial of Wilber Hill. Having the extra horses to ride had spared the animal. The first morning out of Des Moines, the bay was impatient to step out. Snorting and bobbing its head, it waited for Oli to finish breaking camp and have one last cup of coffee.

The clouds were thick toward the west and the air smelled of rain. By mid-morning the rain came sweeping across the plains. The sheet of water was punctuated by streaks of lightning. Donning his slicker, and pulling his hat brim down low, Oli continued riding as the rain engulfed them.

It was a real gully washer. Soon, the small streams that had been easy to cross became raging torrents. With care, he guided the bay through the belly-deep water. The sure-footed horse did not hesitate to enter when urged to cross. It was late afternoon when the rain stopped. Heavy cloud cover remained and with the storm came cold wind.

Under the slicker, Oli's wool shirt and pants were soaked. Steam rose off the bay's wet hair. It was time to start looking for a place to spend the night. As they approached a tumbling stream, he decided to stop.

There was little cover on the plain. Some scrub oak grew along the banks.

Stripping the saddle and blanket from the bay, he set it out on the picket rope. Soon the horse was rolling and enjoying the freedom from its burden. Oli searched along the rushing water, collecting what wood he could find. The soggy clothing gave little comfort against the cool air.

Before long, the sound of a crackling fire lifted his spirits. His wet clothes hung on some low brush and he put on his spare outfit from the saddlebags. With the bay rubbed down and hot coffee on the fire, he felt almost human. He had stopped a couple of hours before dark, so it was a good night to cook a meal of beans. Adding some generous slices of salt pork to the boiling pot, he sat back and sipped strong coffee.

"Hello, the fire. You got room for a drowned traveler?"

Looking up, Oli saw a buckskin-covered rider on a tired-looking sorrel. He was leading a buckskin with a pack. After making sure his Colt was within reach just in case, he called back, "Have a seat near the fire. Got hot coffee and some beans cooking."

He watched as the old gent stripped the gear from his horses and put them on a picket rope. He walked with a rolling gait and had a big smile on his face.

Grunting, he sat next to the fire and began to warm his hands. "Was mighty glad to see your fire. With all the rain, I weren't lookin' forward to settin' up a camp."

Oli took care to take stock of the new comer.

Pouring coffee into the man's tin cup, he noted the gnarled, well-calloused hands. They were hands that spoke of hard work.

"Thanks," he said, taking a drink of the hot brew. "The name's Henry Stall. On my way ta the fort. Getting stocked up on goods. Will be headin' for the plains ta hunt buffalo."

"Good to meet you, Henry. I'm Oli August. I'm headed for the fort to help out my brother-in-law."

With introductions out of the way, the two sat watching the beans boil while drinking coffee. Oli had some hard biscuits to go with the beans. Soon, both men had plates filled and were shoveling food into their mouths. The hard biscuits were soaked in the juice and were most satisfying.

With bellies full, they sat with some more coffee and talked about the plains and hunting. Henry enjoyed telling stories about his trips. He had traveled through much of the territory east of the Rocky Mountains, harvesting buffalo hides. Oli had made the trip to the mountains nine years prior and was familiar with much of the area. He still found the stories interesting and made note of places he had not been that Henry had traveled.

With the fire burning low and the horses checked on, the two men spread their blankets over ground covers. The clouds had cleared and the stars stood out in the night sky. Oli pulled his blankets around his shoulders and laid there thinking about Fort Leavenworth. He knew that there was a possibility that Martin might be guilty of the crimes he was charged with. Even if he believed his brother-in-law was innocent, he might not be able to do anything to help him.

With the hooting sounds of an owl somewhere along the tumbling stream, Oli dozed off into dreamless sleep. Henry Stall added a bit of security to traveling the lonely roads to the fort.

Morning found the stream down and the sky bright blue. The chill in the air made it more invigorating. Oli hopped around in his stocking feet and he pulled his boots on. He was just two days from the fort and anxious to get back on the road.

"Slow down my, friend," Henry said. "We'll have a good breakfast of leftover beans and coffee before headin' out."

Looking at the old trapper, he knew that it was good advice. Too often the meals were less than satisfying, without much staying power.

"I got some salt pork left we can fry up. It will be a meal fit for a king." Oli began to put kindling on last night's ashes, coaxing some of the remaining coals back into flames.

Grunting as he stood up, Henry went to water the horses and put them on new grass. Happy for the attention, they snorted and stomped in the cool morning air.

With breakfast cooked, they ate and Henry commented that beans always tasted better after being warmed up. Using sand along the stream bank to scour the pans, soon things were packed and the horses stomped with anticipation of getting underway.

Again the sun brought out the bright colors of the rolling plains, even more lush from the rain the day before. They passed a farm with a sod house and split rail corral. A woman with two small children knelt at a stream doing laundry. A man plowing the tough grassland with two mules waved at them as they rode by.

Pangs of loneliness went through Oli as he looked at the family. He should be home with Joan right now instead of on the road. He missed sitting with her and having coffee in the morning, or watching the Turkey River flow by in the evening dusk.

CHAPTER FOUR

The fort was on the west bank of the Missouri River, situated on a series of bluffs to prevent potential flooding. Fort Leavenworth was the staging point of the western army currently fighting a war with Mexico. It also had been used in prior years against the Cherokees, with as many as 20 companies of dragoons.

The fort was busy with freight wagons hauling supplies from the steamboat landing, wagon trains camping on the outskirts while resupplying for their trip west, the army troops drilling or assembling to ride out on operations.

They parted as Henry headed for a saloon just outside the fort. With a quick wave, he rode out of Oli's life. It was time to find Martin. The fort consisted of several military buildings within a defendable area and other civilian structures spreading beyond. It took several inquiries before Oli was directed to the guardhouse.

A surly sergeant sat at a time-worn desk in the

front office. Several closed doors led to inner offices. A low railing split the room, keeping visitors in a designated area. There were benches along the wall with a few tired-looking men waiting and talking low amongst themselves. Sitting alone was a young woman in a rather plain-looking dress, a bonnet covering her hair and face.

Oli approached the rail. "Excuse me. Is it possible to see Martin Maier?"

Without looking up, the sergeant pushed a log book toward him. It had a pencil tethered to it. "Fill out your name and reason for visit. Then wait on the benches for approval. If you can't write, sit on the bench and I will arrange a clerk to fill it out for you. Any weapons must be left on the desk."

The sergeant then looked up with a blank look, waiting to see what Oli did. Taking the book, Oli filled in his name and an explanation for his visit. He had left his guns and knife with his gear at the livery. Setting the book back on the desk, he waited a moment. Looking up again, the sergeant took the book and waved him away to sit down.

There was an impressive three-day clock on the wall that said it was 11:00 a.m. Turning, he sat on the uncomfortable bench. A corporal came in from one of the inner rooms and looked over the book, making a couple notes in another log. Thirty minutes later, two of the other men waiting were called and went into a side room which appeared to have a table and several chairs. There were guards on each end. The door closed quietly behind them. There was the sound of a lock being turned.

He looked over at the young lady. She sat with

her head turned away from him. Oli sat, thinking about the long ride from Elkader and how much more comfortable the saddle was compared to the hard bench. Slowly, each one was called to go into the side room. It was after 2:00 p.m. when his name was called.

The straight-backed chairs were no more comfortable than the bench. He sat and watched the guard at one end of the room summon Martin from a holding cell just out of sight.

"You're a busy man today, lieutenant. You have another visitor."

He opened the door and Martin Maier walked in, wearing a uniform that showed signs of being worn too many days between cleaning. He had lost weight since Oli had last seen him and his face was pale. Despite his appearance, a broad smile came to his face when he saw his company.

"Oli, Oli August, am I glad to see you." Quickly, he moved across the room and grasped his hand.

"Joan sends her love. She is . . . we are worried about you. Your letter did not say much."

Sitting across from Oli, Martin sat with his hands spread on the table. "I really don't know where to start. First off, I am being framed for the robbery and killing. I was in charge of the payroll. It was stolen and my sergeant guarding the payroll during my absence was killed. I was found north of the fort, on the military road, unconscious after the robbery and cannot tell you how I got there."

Oli listened while Martin recounted the events that he remembered from that night. He had locked the payroll, which was gold and silver coins, in his office safe. When the payroll was in his charge, he would sleep on a bunk just off the office. A guard would be posted just outside the office.

That evening, he had locked up the payroll like usual. He had been invited to have dinner with an acquaintance who had just come in on a steamboat. The person had insisted on the meeting because they would only be staying one night and leaving the next morning.

Sergeant Klaus had been standing guard that night. Martin had worked with the sergeant for over a year and had considered him competent and trustworthy. Making an exception to having a meal brought in because of the payroll, he had decided to have an early meal with the acquaintance. After letting the sergeant know where he would be, he had gone to the Donner House.

Dinner had lasted about two hours. After the meal, the acquaintance had insisted on a brandy. He had then bid his company farewell and had returned to the office. Sergeant Klaus was at his post and had assured him all was well. Martin had remembered being very tired when he'd gotten back. He'd opened the safe to check on the payroll. He had remembered seeing the money, but that was all.

He had woken up the next day, surrounded by troops from the fort holding guns on him. There was a severe bruise on his temple and he had been lying on the side of the road.

He was told that the sergeant had been found dead outside the office by the relief watch. The payroll was gone and the trail of his horse and a pack horse had been followed to this part of the road. It was surmised that the horses had been startled in the dark and Martin thrown. The animals had run toward the Missouri River, where the trail was lost. It appeared they had run into the river and were washed downstream. Martin's horse had been found a couple of miles below the entry point. The packhorse was found a day later across the river, without its rig. It was figured that it had slipped off while the horse struggled in the water.

The guard walked over to the two men. "Yer time's up, lieutenant."

Oli got up, his mind spinning from the information Martin had given him. The second guard held the door for him to leave. Stopping, Oli turned back to Martin.

"Who was the acquaintance? Do you know where he is?"

"Yes, I do. It is a she and she came in just before you. Her name is Angela Russo."

Upset that they were still talking after being told the time was up, the guard grabbed Martin and pushed him toward the holding cell.

It was after 4:00 p.m. when Oli stepped out of the guardhouse. Halfway across the street, he looked back at the formidable stone building. He could forget about busting Martin out. It was time to find a place to spend the night. He headed for a boarding house not far from the livery.

A woman in a stained apron met him at the door. Her arms were covered with flour and bits of dough. "Yes, we have an open room," she said, squinting her eyes, looking him over carefully.

"Be four bits a day, which includes breakfast. Another long bit if you want supper included."

"Thank you. I'll take the room." Oli had missed the mid-day meal and his stomach growled with anticipation of a meal. "Include supper, please."

He didn't know how long he would be at the fort, but 65 cents per day including meals was a good price. That is, if the lady in front of him could cook.

Wiping the flour from her arms, she walked toward a sideboard with a log book, which looked much like the one he had seen at the guardhouse. "Pay in advance, sign in or make your mark. How long you be staying?"

Giving her some coins, he said, "Two nights for sure. If it is okay, I will let you know then."

"Top of the stairs, second room on the left," she said, grabbing the coins and turning back towards the kitchen. Over her shoulder she called, "Chicken and biscuits tonight at six. Supper is over at seven."

The room was sparsely furnished. The bed was little more than a cot. A pitcher with water and a bowl sat on a low table. A small window with a sack cloth curtain faced the street. There were only a few feet on each side of the bed. Standing out from the rest of the room was a rather nice woven red rug on the floor.

He headed back to the livery to gather his gear. The hostler named Digger saw him walk in.

"Moved your gear into the feed room. Didn't want someone coming in and walking off with it."

"Appreciate it, Digger. I got a room at the boarding house up the street."

"Ma Walker's place? She is a fair cook. Heard

she has a fine room with a red carpet. Haven't seen it myself."

Nodding and smiling, Oli picked up his gear, leaving the saddle and blanket hanging on the rack near the bay's stall. He noticed that the horse had plenty of hay and had already been given grain.

He had just enough time to stow his gear and wash up before supper. Five other men were seated at the table when he arrived. Ma Walker served a supper well worth the long bit. A big pan of chicken and biscuits was place in the center of the table. A wicker basket with additional biscuits was next to it with a bowl of butter. There were some carrots and parsnips in the gravy mixture. It lacked a bit for meat, but with plenty of gravy and biscuits, one could not complain. There was a mug of buttermilk for each, followed by coffee. Warm cornbread with molasses was served as dessert.

"Had apple pie yesterday," a portly boarder boasted. "I ate two pieces with cheese."

"Sorry I missed the pie," Oli said, thinking about the dried apples he had brought home for Joan.

"You got that nice room with the red carpet, didn't you?" the man continued. "Had it myself last trip," he said around a big bite of cornbread.

The other boarders ate their meals in silence. Two of them he recognized from the guardhouse. His chunky new friend kept up a constant chatter until the meal was done. No doubt he was a drummer like Sal. *Must be you need a gift of gab for the job,* Oli thought.

With supper over and the sun low in the west, he decided to visit some of the local saloons to see if he could pick up any info on the robbery.

He walked into a place with the sound of an inviting piano. He remembered another time on the Ohio River and a piano player named Jinx. Entering the saloon, he stopped for a moment, glancing back at the setting sun shining through the fly-specked window.

Blinking, he let his eyes adjust to the low lighting. He had left his guns in the room, but carried the Good Knife in its sheath at the nape of his neck. The place was almost empty. Two teamsters sat at a table sharing a bottle of rye after a day of hauling freight. A short, skinny man in a waistcoat banged away at the piano. The bartender was a tall, stocky man with hair plastered down with grease. His creased face showed years of working in the sun before getting a job indoors.

Stepping up to the bar, Oli ordered a rye. Pouring the drink quickly and splashing as much on the bar, the bartender turned back to what he was doing. Taking a sip, the hot amber liquid burned all the way down. He liked the way it warmed his belly, but knew too much belly warming could get him in trouble. A couple of soldiers came in and stepped up to the bar next to him.

After a bit, he asked them about the payroll robbery. The taller, red-faced man snarled, "That damn Maier took our payroll and we had to wait two extra weeks to get paid. He killed poor old Sergeant Klaus. Crushed his skull like a melon. Never knew what hit him. Now the skunk sits in cool comfort in the officers' section of the guardhouse, waiting for the army to decide prison or hanging."

The short, pock-marked soldier chimed in,

"They best hang him and do it slow."

It started conversation between the soldiers and teamsters. It was basically negative toward Martin. There was no doubt in these men's minds that the lieutenant was guilty.

He was just about to leave and search elsewhere for information when the batwing doors flew open with a loud bang. In walked a large, drunk and angry hulk of a man who swaggered up to the bar. Pounding his massive fist on the planks, he demanded a bottle.

Oli watched as the soldiers ducked out the door to find a safer place to drink. The teamsters turned their backs to the arrival and ignored him. The bartender grabbed a bottle and glass, placing them in front of the big man.

"Four bits, Bart. Take it easy on the furniture," the bartender growled.

Finishing his drink, Oli thought back to his last trip out west. He had met a bruiser named Bart Nevell. He had barely finished the thought when a rough hand grabbed him. He turned and was looking up into the face of the man.

"Have a drink with me," he snorted, spewing putrid breath.

With mixed feelings, he realized that the man was indeed Bart Nevell. A good man when sober, trouble when drunk. He had stolen Oli's shoes on their first meeting.

"I would be happy to drink with you, Mr. Nevell," he replied.

Hearing his last name spoken stopped Bart for

a moment. Through the drunken haze, he wondered if he knew this blond man next to him.

Oli stepped back and poured himself a drink from Bart's bottle. Holding it up for a toast he said, "To Jack Albert's wagon train."

The man remembered a trip years back where he scouted for a man named Albert. Jutting his chin out, he looked at the little man next to him.

"Oli, I am Oli August."

Slowly, recognition came to Bart's face and then a crooked grin. A large hand slapped him on the back, nearly knocking his wind out.

"I borrowed your shoes one time. Hell, you saved my bacon when the Indians had me trapped under my horse."

Wanting to put space between himself and his sour-smelling friend, Oli suggested they sit at a table and talk over old times.

Bart rambled on about the wagon train, telling the same stories over and over while tossing down shots of rye. Taking care to drink slowly while pretending otherwise, he let the man talk. The saloon had begun to fill up with soldiers. The two from earlier had returned.

The rye was quickly taking effect on the big man. It was doubtful that he would be able to walk out. Oli left for a moment to relieve himself out back. When he returned, the back door was stuck and he could hear shouts and the splintering of chairs inside.

Running around to the front, he barely dodged a soldier tumbling out the door. In the middle of the room, Bart stood, trying to fight off several soldiers.

He watched as the tall, red-faced soldier raised his dragoon to club Bart. Like a flash, Oli drew the Good Knife and sent it slicing through the man's upraised arm. Yelping, he let the gun drop to the sawdust-covered floor. Suddenly, a shotgun blast rocked the room.

Through the haze he saw the bartender holding the smoking scatter gun. The fighting soldiers ducked away, releasing Bart, who staggered and fell to the floor.

"There's another barrel left. Now get your saggy backsides out of my saloon," he commanded the cowering soldiers.

Stumbling over each other, soldiers left the saloon, leaving Bart lying on the floor, and the tall, red-faced man leaning against the bar holding his bleeding arm. Oli walked up to him and pulled the Good Knife loose, wiping it on the man's shirt. The bartender walked around the bar and wrapped a rag around the wound.

Pushing the wounded soldier in front of him, the bartender sent him out the batwing doors. He then turned to Oli. "You best get your drunken friend the hell out of here. He's been sticking up for that Lieutenant Maier, and these soldiers don't like it. They'll be back with others and won't be liking you much, either."

With the help of the bartender, Oli got Bart to his feet and out the door. They were less than a hundred paces from the livery stable. He figured that it would be the best place to bring the man to sleep it off. Wet with sweat from trying to guide the stumbling hulk, he finally got to the livery door. Digger met him at the door and help guide the bruiser to a pile of hay, where they dropped the burden.

Shaking his head, Digger looked at the man. "He has been drunk for a week. The army let him go over some disagreement about that lieutenant and he has been drinking ever since. Thought he would run out of money before now."

The hostler went back to watering the horses. Gasping for breath, Oli sat looking down at his old friend. He wondered what made him think Martin was innocent. He would have to wait for Bart to sober up for that answer.

He headed back toward the boarding house with the all-too-familiar snoring coming from Bart. He washed his hands and rinsed his face before turning in. Settling onto the cot, he felt the leather straps supporting the feather tick cut into his back. The last thing he remembered thinking before falling asleep was that the red carpet on the floor would probably be more comfortable.

* * *

The first light of morning was coming through the small window when Oli woke. Getting up, he looked out and realized he could see the steamboats on the Missouri River from his room. He watched as the majestic black stacks moved past.

He hurried down to the dining room and could hear Ma Walker busy in the kitchen. The chair scraped over the worn floor boards when he sat down.

"Pancakes will be a few more minutes. Bring

in a cup. The coffee is ready," she called from behind the curtain.

Pushing the curtain aside, he walked in, the heat of the cook stove in the small kitchen hitting him in the face. Flushed from the heat, Ma Walker was mixing a bowl of batter. The stove was covered with a thick sheet of metal that had melting lard crackling on it. The steaming coffee pot sat near the edge of the stove.

Using a rag lying nearby to hold the pot, he poured a cup of the hardy brew. He watched as she ladled four large oval pancakes onto the grease-covered sheet.

She nodded at the cupboard behind him. "Got some honey in the tin there and a bowl of butter. Bring them out to the table for me and I'll be right along with your cakes."

Thanking her, he went back to the table and sat to enjoy the morning coffee. His mouth had a bit of a cottony feeling, even though he had not drank a lot of rye the night before.

Smiling quite proudly at the stack of cakes, she came out from behind the curtain and placed the plate in front of him.

"These sourdough griddle cakes will keep you going till supper." Laughing, she headed back to the kitchen.

He was just stuffing the last forkful of the cakes, sweetened with honey and dripping with butter, into his mouth when the portly peddler came in. Nodding to the man, Oli gulped his coffee, washing them down.

The peddler, eyes dancing with excitement, called to the kitchen, "I smell pancakes!"

"Set yourself down and I'll be right out with a stack for you."

Oli pointed to the coffee pot sitting on a heated stone on the sideboard. Taking a last sip from the cup, he nodded and headed out of the dining room, leaving the hungry man anticipating his stack of cakes.

Taking the stairs two at a time, he went up to his room and got his revolver. Settling the holster on his hip, he double-checked the knife at the nape of his neck. Ready, he headed for the stable.

Digger had the coffee on the potbelly stove and was filling a cup for Bart, who sat against a stall holding his head in his hands. The foul smell of the large man's body greeted Oli as he came in. Despite having seen the man drunk before, he could not ever remember seeing him in this disheveled condition.

He lifted his head and looked at the blond man. Then, letting his head fall back against the stall, he closed his eyes.

"Got you some coffee here, Bart," the hostler said, pressing the cup of coffee into the large hand. "You wake up now. You have a man here that needs to talk to you,"

Grunting, the bruiser took the cup and tasted it. "Awful stuff you make. If the rye doesn't kill me, your coffee sure will."

Digger laughed and picked up a fork to give hay to the stock. "Once you clear your head, you can help me clean these stalls to pay for your night's stay."

Oli sat impatiently, waiting for Bart to drink

enough coffee to think straight. Finally, after the second cup he tilted his head back and looked up.

"How are you doing, Oli?"

"Not so good, Bart. I am here because of my brother-in-law, Lieutenant Maier. I want to look into the robbery and murder."

"Weren't robbery or murder, from what I found," Bart declared. "He was framed. Course, nobody wants to believe me."

Oli stood up and sniffed the brew in the coffee pot. Bart was right. It was yesterday's grounds with more water. Deciding against having a cup, he turned to Bart.

"Why do you believe he's innocent?"

The bruiser cleared his throat. "The sign did not agree with the story. After the payroll went missing, I went to look for it while the tracks were still fresh. The two horses left the fort traveling just west of the Military Road. The tracks were wrong. The packhorse should have been carrying a bigger load and had deeper tracks. Turns out the lead horse was carrying more weight."

"The trail came to the road and got mixed in other tracks going back and forth. Where the lieutenant was found the tracks of the two horses went running hard towards the river. The load on the horses was less. The trail ran into the river and disappeared. I figure someone swum them out into the river and then released them."

"Did you bring this to the attention of the commander?" Oli interrupted.

"Not for a few days," Bart continued. "I spent

three days searching for any sign that may be a heavily loaded packhorse. Or even a loaded, ridden horse that left the road. Working up and down the road, I finally found where some horses had been held a couple miles back toward the fort. It was between the road and the robbers' trail. I found the same tracks of four horses leaving the road about six hours south of the fort. I figured they waited for whoever brought the gold and silver from the fort and then, after sending the horses into the river, they rode through the night before leaving the road and camping."

"I was out of grub by that time and had to come back to the fort to resupply. I caught hell for being gone while searching for the trail. They said I was as bad as a deserter. I had missed a patrol I was supposed to scout for."

Bart sat a moment, frowning, looking as though he was remembering something distasteful. A man in the west was only as good as his word. To be labeled anything else was not easy to live with.

"What did they say when you finally told them what you found?" Oli inquired.

"Simple, they said I was reading something into the sign that was not there. The lieutenant's horse and the pack horse had been found downstream as expected. Only the lieutenant and the commander had the combination to the safe. Nobody else could have gotten to the payroll."

"I have to find the payroll," Oli stated as he paced the dusty livery floor.

"Not finding it has kept your brother-in-law from hanging. They are hoping he hid the payroll somewhere and need to keep him alive to find out where."

"Whoever has the money is a month ahead of us. For all we know the coins are already spent," Oli worried.

"Unlikely they spent it. These coins minted for the payroll were dated and stamped with FL for Fort Leavenworth. They will be easy to trace once spent. I figure whoever has them will wait until fighting between us and Mexico is over and then they'll head south to live like kings."

Again getting a smell of Bart's filthy attire, Oli stepped back. "I have to do some checking around the fort and try and see Martin again. Why don't you go take a bath and get into some clean clothes? We can meet tomorrow morning and make plans on how to find the payroll."

"I am a bit ripe, alright." Bart paused before continuing. "I knew you would come. The lieutenant told me you married his sister when I talked of you one time. It was good to learn you hadn't died in the wilderness."

The tender side of Bart did not show often. Oli nodded, not trusting his voice, and walked out of the stable.

He went back to the guardhouse. It took two hours to get in to see Martin. His brother-in-law's face was pale. Something had changed since their last meeting.

Sitting heavily on the chair across from Oli, Martin spoke. "They scheduled my hanging in two weeks. I just got the word this morning."

Shocked at the news, Oli sat back and felt his

breakfast turn in his stomach. With his mind racing, he told his brother-in-law about meeting Bart and what had been said. He took care to keep his voice low so the guards couldn't hear. Also, he let Martin know that the two of them would be going to find the men who had the payroll.

Martin cautioned him, "These are ruthless men you are looking for. I believe they meant to leave me for dead, thinking my head was crushed like the sergeant's. My injury was supposed to look like a fall from the startled horse."

For a moment, the two men sat in silence. Then, Martin looked into Oli's eyes with a serious stare that sent chills down his spine. "Angela does not know about the date for hanging. You've got to let her know."

"Where can I find Angela?" Oli asked.

"She is staying with the mayor's family. Anyone can point the house out for you." Martin grasped Oli's hands and continued. "You know, she stayed rather than going back east when she learned about my arrest. Angela is the only person that I have been able to confide in. Even my lawyer believed I was guilty. I had met her on a previous trip to New Orleans. Angela had just arrived the day of the robbery. We had so little time together."

"Can you trust her?" Oli asked.

"With my life. I love her, Oli."

Leaving the guardhouse, he stood squinting in the bright sunshine. Desperately, he tried to organize his thoughts. Something to write on was needed to plan. The two week deadline was unexpected and had left Oli shaken.

A small shop a short distance from the guardhouse caught his attention. It sold eastern newspapers and other reading material. Stepping in, he could smell the ink from the papers mixed with the mustiness of used books. He was pleased to find a tally book and wooden pencils.

Clutching a tally book and two pencils, he headed for the livery. Bart was just finishing up helping Digger clean the stalls. A new layer of sweat had been added to the soiled clothes.

Laughing at the look Oli gave him. Bart said, "I know what you are thinking. I am just heading out for that bath. I already had some clothes washed."

"Martin's hanging is scheduled in two weeks," Oli blurted out.

"Damn," Bart exclaimed and threw down the fork. "Got to go, we got a lot to do tomorrow to get ready to leave." With that, he headed out to get cleaned up.

It was unbelievable when comparing the drunk and sober Bart. He vowed to keep him sober. After checking on his horse and gear, it was time to look up Angela Russo. The house was quickly found from Digger's description.

The stately white building with prominent columns in the front stood out from the other houses in the area. Oli knocked on the door and it was answered by a black servant. He was escorted into the library. The rich, dark wooden shelves were lined with books, more than he had ever seen in one place.

The elegant lady who came into the room looked nothing like the plain, bonneted person sitting on a bench in the guardhouse. She wore a crisp, flowing dress that accented her waist and bosom. Her hair hung in perfect ringlets and the top was held in place with some type of silver clasp.

This is what a southern lady looks like, he thought. Standing quickly, he felt under-dressed in his wool shirt and pants. Gripping his hat with both hands, he stared at her

Holding her hand out, she said, "I am Angela Russo, and you must be Oli August."

Her voice was like velvet. Awkwardly, he stepped forward and took her hand briefly. For a moment, he suspected she was enjoying his uneasiness.

"It is a pleasure meeting you. Martin . . . Lieutenant Maier asked me to see you," he stammered.

"I am so worried about him. He was so sad during our visit yesterday. Maybe your being here will help him get through what is happening."

Oli felt her words were right, but her eyes lacked emotion.

"I appreciate the support you have been giving him," he said, following her lead. "Martin got some bad news today. They've scheduled his hanging in two weeks."

There was a small gasp as she turned away. With her hands covering her mouth, she turned back to him with large, unblinking eyes. "I am so sorry. This can't happen."

Moving to a silk-covered chair, Angela sat heavily and stared at the floor. Unsure of what to do next, Oli stood in silence.

Standing quickly, her composure back, she took a step toward Oli. "I'm sorry, I forgot my manners. Can we do anything to make your stay at Fort Leavenworth more comfortable?" she asked.

Confused by the sudden recovery and the question, he looked into the now cold, dark eyes. "I am staying at a boarding house just up from Digger's Livery. I will be leaving the day after tomorrow, but I do appreciate the offer."

The remaining visit was not long and he learned little from her. She excused herself due to a prior engagement.

Oli was relieved to be back on the street. It felt great to be away from the uncomfortable environment. He had no desire to move in their society or spend time with them. He was most comfortable enjoying a meal in a place like Ma Walker's. In fact, that was where he was heading. It was almost 6:00 and time for supper.

Bart showed up right after breakfast dressed in clean, though slightly worn, clothes. He had a revolver and military-style holster on his right hip. A flap secured the gun in place. His woolen breeches were tucked into calf-high boots. A knife handle protruded from the top of the left boot.

First, a trip to resupply was necessary. A trading post just out of town was suggested. The men were in no hurry riding after supplies. Oli wanted to spend time committing the terrain around the fort to memory. Arriving at the low building, they tied the horses to a worn and well-chewed rail. Walking in, the men were greeted with the smell of new leather and oiled steel traps. The shelves were lined with goods necessary for a man to travel in the wild country.

Oli handed the stoop-shouldered proprietor a page from his tally book with the list of items he needed. Flashing a toothless smile, the man turned quickly and began putting items into burlap bags. While he watched the man load the supplies, Bart looked over slickers and blankets.

A fine display of hunting knives was on one wall. The Good Knife had been a fine weapon. It was excellent for throwing. Oli decided to get another for cleaning game or general cutting.

Loaded down with two bags of supplies and a new knife on Oli's hip, the men emerged from the low building. The wind had picked up and was blowing in thunderheads from the west. Oli returned to the livery to store his supplies while Bart ran a few other errands.

Digger offered him a cup of coffee. Knowing Digger's coffee wasn't the best, Oli decided the hot brew would help ward off the chill that was settling into the area. Sipping the weak brew, he watched as the hostler worked at repairing a broken harness.

"Thanks for the coffee," Oli said to break the silence.

"You know, Mr. August, most folks think your brother-in-law is guilty." Pulling the leather strap on the harness to evaluate the repair, he looked Oli in the eye. "I myself am not sure whose story is true. The lieutenant appears to be a good man. Bart holds stock in his version of what happened. We may never know for sure if he is innocent or not."

Oli felt a chill at the thought that Martin could be guilty. The thought that he could have committed such a violent crime was unthinkable. He came from the same stock as Joan. They shared the same values.

"I know it appears that the trial was correct," Oli said, "but I know Martin's character and his upbringing. To steal, and even worse, to kill in the act of stealing would be impossible for him to do."

"Maybe so," Digger replied.

The response didn't carry the conviction Oli would have liked to hear. It was time to go and visit Martin once again before heading out. Turning up his collar to cut the wind on his neck, he headed toward the guardhouse.

Three sour-looking soldiers lounged in front of the door. Oli felt the hair stand on the back of his neck as the men turned toward him as he approached. He was forced to stop short of the doorway. Standing as tall as his 5' 8" frame would allow, he steeled himself for the coming confrontation.

"Stand aside, gentlemen. I am here to visit the lieutenant," he said in a cold, flat tone. He felt his biceps flex involuntarily in preparation to fight.

"Watch this one. He carries a knife," the ruddy-faced soldier warned. Being off duty, none of the men carried a weapon.

"The knife won't do ya no good when the hangman is done with your lieutenant," a chubby private snorted.

Slowly, they stepped aside, delaying him as much as possible without escalating the situation. A young, blond private was the last to get out of his way. As Oli entered the guardhouse, there was sweat on his forehead caused from the adrenaline racing through his veins.

The visit was short and Martin appeared agitated. Oli assured him that he would make every effort to discover the real culprit and, if possible, return with the gold.

As he left, he felt less confident than he had tried to sound inside. He was depending heavily on Bart to help him on his quest. Before he returned to the boarding house, he needed to send a telegraph to Joan. His stomach tightened as he pondered what message he would send.

Trusting Bart to be ready to leave at daylight the next morning, he didn't look for him before returning to the boarding house. Supper was on the table when he arrived. There was buffalo stew with freshly baked bread. The portly guest had left after breakfast. The others at supper had little to say. It was just as well. He had lots to think about. The stew was followed by some kind of cake with wild strawberries poured over each piece. Oli vowed to remember this and tell Joan about it once he got home.

Before turning in, he walked down to the livery and stowed everything except his revolver, knife and the clothes on his back. Returning to his room, he noticed that the carpet was gone. There was a tap on his door. Ma Walker stepped in and directed him to go to the last room down the hall.

"It has more room, a better bed, and I moved the carpet."

Leaving him in the new room, she proudly went back down the stairs. Oli was impressed with the room. It was a little larger, had a bigger window, and was closer to the toilet. And, of course, it now had the red carpet.

He spent the next hour jotting down notes in the tally book. A clear plan did not develop. Finally, with his eyes aching from staring at the book, he decided that a fresh look in the morning might help. Setting the book onto a small table next to the overstuffed bed, he burrowed his head into the feather pillow and forced his mind to stop pondering the problem.

Oli had barely drifted to sleep when he was woken by a commotion downstairs. There were several loud male voices and Ma Walker yelling at them. Pulling his clothes on quickly, he poked his head out of the door.

There were soldiers looking for someone. Could it be friends of the man he had stuck with the Good Knife? Ma Walker was arguing loudly with them that there was no such man in her boarding house. Stepping into the hall, Oli cracked the door to the back stairs. In the low light, he could see two men standing at the bottom. He recognized the young blond private. Carefully, he closed the door.

Moving back into the room he opened the window. Behind him he heard loud boots on the stairs. Turning his back to the window, he drew his revolver. A door crashed open. It was the room he had slept in last night! If they had checked the log downstairs it would have said that room.

Without hesitation, he holstered his revolver and crawled out the window. Then, dropping to the ground and keeping to the shadows, he moved around the next building and headed for the livery. A man stepped in front of him. Oli reached for his gun and felt a powerful hand grab his arm.

"It's me!" Bart hissed. "They sent a man to check for your horse at the livery. He is now sleeping in my bed of hay. I got the horses and gear and figured

I better find you before more men show up at Digger's."

The two men led their animals away from the fort under the cover of darkness. Oli walked, wondering why they were so intent on finding him. He wondered if Angela might be involved. Maybe she had told them where he was staying.

CHAPTER FIVE

A hazy morning brought light to two exhausted men sleeping in an old buffalo wallow just off the Military Road. They had only been there for three hours. Their horses were picketed nearby for quick access. It was fully daylight before one of them moved.

Oli raised his head and took a moment to remember why he was there. Sitting in the damp chill of the dawn, he recalled their flight from Fort Leavenworth with soldiers searching for him. Bart knew the best way to get away without being spotted. After leading their horses a half-mile south, they had mounted and had taken the Military Road south. It was the best way to obscure their tracks. A good tracker could sort theirs from the many others, but he had the best tracker at the fort with him. The heavy cloud cover had been in their favor, masking their movements.

The fire was going and the coffee on when Bart

sat up and stretched. "What's for breakfast?" he inquired.

"I'm making a pot of Digger's coffee," Oli responded.

Lying back down and pulling up his blanket, Bart muttered, "In that case, I will keep on sleeping."

"You take care of the horses. I will fry us up some bacon to go with Ma Walker's biscuits."

Reluctantly, Bart rolled up his blankets and headed out to check on the stock. Oli watched him lead the bay and the sturdy-looking buckskin to the small stream near the wallow. Returning from his chores, he was greeted with the smell of boiling coffee and crackling bacon.

It was mid-morning when they arrived at the spot where Bart had found their camp on his prior search. The tracks were long gone, washed out by several storms over the past month. Only the unburned wood of the old fire and discarded trash was left.

Shaking his head, Oli stared at the old site. "Not much to see. Sure doesn't tell us much."

Bart dismounted and squatted near the cold fire pit. "I don't agree. How a man sets up his camp is the same from one to another. I look at the set up and trash. When you follow a man long enough, you always know if he has stopped in a place by what is left behind. In some cases it takes years for the sign to disappear."

With that he picked up an empty tin can, looked at it and tossed it aside. Oli watched as he finished circling the area.

"I was here when the camp was fresh. At that time I was close on their heels and more concerned with finding marks of their boots and horse shoes. I didn't look for much around the camp."

Oli watched the big man with fascination. He remembered learning much from him on the wagon train. He realized the man had much more to teach. He was fortunate to have him on their side.

Leaving the abandoned site, they continued south. It was unlikely that anyone from the fort would be pursuing them. It was also doubtful that the raid at the boarding house had been ordered by anyone in authority. A knife incident would not cause such a stir. A group of vengeful troops would.

The sun burned through the haze and was shining brightly as they followed the road. There were log bridges over the streams. Dirt had been spread over the logs to improve the surface for horses. Logs had been laid to create passage on marshy ground. Trees had been removed in the wooded areas to allow defendable travel for army troops. Oli had a sinking feeling, despite the beautiful day. Somewhere south of them were the men who had the payroll. They could be holed up anywhere and easily missed. Were they out on the plains or in one of the small towns? There was less than two weeks, and too much territory to search.

The rhythm of the bay under him as it walked had a lulling effect and he had to fight the urge to close his eyes and doze. Bart rode alongside, straight and square in the saddle, his eyes watching the surrounding landscape.

Oli shook his head to clear his mind. Having a

man like Bart riding with you tended to allow you to become more lax. You depend on the other to be on watch and warn you of danger. He knew that two men see more than one. He also needed to study the terrain for future reference. Right now they were riding on an improved road. More than likely, they would have to leave it soon.

"Got to watch for Mexicans or Indians," Bart said unexpectedly. "We are in a fight with Mexico. They send patrols out now and again. Sometimes they stir up some of the Cherokee or Osage, getting them to raid travelers."

The warning did not go unheeded. Oli sat up straighter and was more vigilant about their surroundings.

The two stopped for a midday meal. Cold biscuits and water from their canteens made up the fare. To the east was the Missouri River, with its many tributaries flowing into it. These were surrounded by various types of trees, brush, and brambles. To the west were the rolling plains. Some of the plain was covered with coarse buffalo grass, while other areas were more sparsely covered and had low shrubs, including mesquite and catclaw.

To the west was the Santa Fe Trail, which wound through desert and high cliffs of sandstone carved into various shapes by the wind.

"If the goal is to go into Mexico, where would they find a place to hole up until traveling is safer?" Oli asked, more of himself than his big companion.

"Good question," Bart replied.

Wrinkling his brow, he looked south and then at Oli. "I have been down this road as far as Fort

Gibson. It is a good 10 days' ride. Fort Scott is four days. Beyond Fort Gibson is Texas or Mexican territory. Between here and Gibson there is plenty of trouble with the tribes and Mexicans."

"That would mean they would have to head for an area that had our soldiers. The Mexican war could go on for years," Oli added.

"Worse yet," Bart said, "we don't know who we are looking for."

He was right. They could be in the same town and pass them on the street and not know. Suddenly, Oli had a thought.

"To get in and out of the fort without being noticed, some of the men would have to be military. They would want to stay near the payroll, which means they would have to become deserters. How can we find out who might have done so at the time of the robbery?"

Oli had enemies back at Fort Leavenworth and could not go back and ask questions. Maybe Bart could do so. He was about to suggest it when the big man came up with an idea.

"We go to Fort Scott and ask around. Word is sent down the line on deserters."

They were two days ride from Fort Scott. The bay was in good shape for the trip. Bart's horse looked like it had staying power. With a plan of action, Oli felt a bit better. The word would have been sent a month ago, but the names would be on record.

While they rode, Bart would swing off the road, looking over likely camping spots. One such check brought him galloping back. "Found something, Oli!"

With that, he wheeled the buckskin and rode back to the west side of the road.

He stopped short of the bank of a shallow stream. A large live oak shaded the area and one of the large branches was broken, lying away from the stream.

Swinging down from his horse, Bart looked over the camp. There was a good-sized fire pit. To the left side of the camp was a pile of rubbish. The large, broken branch had been used as a hitching post. Some poles lay near the fire. They appeared to have been used to support a lean-to or fly tarp.

Oli stayed clear while Bart moved around the site. From the back of the bay, he made mental notes of items left at the campsite. Finally, Bart waved him in. Whoever had stayed here was not too ambitious. Tin cans, animal bones and hides, liquor bottles, and such lay in a scattered pile within throwing distance from the fire. Several cigar butts lay next to the fire.

"It was them," Bart said with satisfaction. "They left their sign all over the place."

"Well, we know they came this way," Oli said, shoving a can with his boot.

"We know more than that," Bart added. "They ain't been gone more than a week. When they left, there were only two of them and their stock. Part of the stay there was another man with an extra horse."

He had concluded this after checking the area where the horses had been tied. They had kept a watch on the road, using a leaning rock for shelter. Some clear boot prints remained. Bart recognized them from before. Oli committed them to memory for the future.

"Found where they may have hid the payroll,"

Bart said, waving Oli over.

A short distance from the camp lay three rocks. They had been rolled away and a hole remained in the center. Piles of dirt lay among the rocks.

Oli had learned at the fort that the payroll was a combination of gold and silver coins. Most of it was silver. The total weight was a little over 140 pounds. It would be too bulky to carry around and would have to be hidden or divided between the men.

They swung up on their horses and rode south for another hour before stopping. Camp was made on a small peninsula at the bend of a creek. It was surrounded by a pecan grove. While Bart took care of the horses, Oli got the fire going. They had shot an antelope that afternoon and they set up a spit using green pecan branches. In no time, the coffee was done and the smell of the roasting meat made it almost feel like home.

Their biscuits were gone, so Oli took some of the sourdough starter and mixed it with flour and water. After adding a few more ingredients, he had some bread rising. Adding some salt pork to the fry pan, he got a nice amount of grease. While they ate the crisp pork, he put bread dough in the pan and fried it golden brown. After the bread was done he poured the remaining grease over the nearly done antelope.

"It is damn near a feast you're making, Oli," Bart said as he took a large bite of the hot bread.

They washed the bread down with coffee while waiting for the meat to be done. Soon, the men were cutting strips of the antelope and skewering them with their knives. The meat had a hint of sage taste, most likely attributed to the brush they had been feeding on.

Both men, being hungry for fresh meat, hardly noticed the gamey flavor.

Sitting with their stomachs full, they sipped coffee and discussed a plan of action. Bart was trimming the remaining meat from the carcass. It would be good for breakfast, or eaten cold at mid-day.

"I think they have traveled to Fort Scott," Oli concluded. "The army would have stopped looking for a deserter that had been gone for a month. They would also need supplies and information on the Mexican war."

"We have a hard day's ride to make the fort," Bart estimated. "I know a guy in the commandant's office that can check on any soldiers from Fort Leavenworth that are missing."

The sun was setting and the western sky was ablaze with color. The men stopped everything and watched it disappear below the horizon. They planned on an early start in the morning, so Oli checked on the horses and then crawled into his blankets. A pack of wolves howled as they chased down some game. Crickets played loudly and night birds called to each other. The night noises were most comforting, and soon both men were sleeping.

CHAPTER SIX

Following along the Marmaton River, the two approached Fort Scott. The fort had been erected five years earlier to help control the relocation of the Indian tribes. It had several civilian businesses outside the fort. One was a single-story hotel which the men chose to stay at. Bart also had his eye on a nearby saloon.

"Bart, can you check with people you know about deserters before hitting the saloon?" Oli asked.

The big man looked at his blond friend with a half-smile. Nodding, he turned the buckskin toward the fort, following a muddy street winding through the scattering of buildings. Some of the construction was rough-sawn lumber. Others were logs. A prominent brick building stood on the bluff overlooking the main fort.

The Lazy Hotel looked like a good place to stay. It had a wooden front and canvas walls in the back. The rooms had plank floors and canvas sides. Two narrow cots and a handmade table with a lamp, bowl and pitcher were the only furniture. Each room had a slab door on leather hinges and a latch string. It offered little security. Finding it acceptable, Oli paid for a room for the two of them. Next, he found a place to put up the horses outside of town. The owner had a small pole building used to board animals. A rock wall ran along the back side of the hotel. It may have been used as a forward defense for the fort.

The lean hotel proprietor smiled as Oli returned from putting up his horse. "There is a decent meal served at Dixie's, just up the street."

"I could use a bath and shave."

Nodding and fussing with some papers on the plank counter, the man replied, "Just south of town, some Osage have set up steam lodges. You got to rinse off in the stream after. Their women give a fair shave."

Shortly, Oli was sitting naked on the floor of a steamy hot lodge. His dirty clothes were being washed and a neatly folded pile of clean clothes were just outside the flap. His tanned face, neck and forearms were in stark contrast with the pale skin on the rest of his body. For the moment, he was back in Finland with the family in their sauna. Sweat dripping down his back and off his forehead was most satisfying.

A young, heavyset woman flipped open the lodge flap and stepped in. Surprised and embarrassed, Oli tried to cover himself. She held up a razor and motioned him to tilt his head up. With skilled hands, she lathered his face and shaved the scrubby beard. With care, she worked around his drooping moustache. Nodding with satisfaction, she headed out of the lodge.

After a cool rinse in the stream, Oli put on his clean clothes. With his revolver back on his hip and the Good Knife on the nape of his neck, he felt dressed. He paid two bits for the steam and shave, and then headed for Dixie's. He had hoped to run into Bart, but did not see him anywhere.

The hotel owner was right, Dixie's served a decent supper. It was served family-style on two long tables. It consisted of a heaping bowl of turnips, roast beef with gravy, and dark bread with a hint of sweet molasses. A bowl of butter sat next to the bread. A steaming-hot pot of coffee sat on a small stove. For dessert there was custard pie.

Oli smiled and thought, *The custard pie gives a promise of eggs in the morning.*

Standing outside the café with a full belly, he looked up and down the street. From this point he could see three saloons. There was a chance that Bart might be in one. First, he checked on his horse. He was pleased to see Bart's horse in the barn. Next, he walked along the muddy street and stopped in the first two establishments. There were several soldiers, some trappers, and a few local men relaxing with card games and enjoying the attention of the colorfully dressed ladies.

The last saloon was the Oak Barrel. It was brightly lit and filled the street with the sound of a tinny piano and a tired-sounding woman singing. Once again, he did not see Bart. Having a drink before turning in sounded good, so he walked up to the scarred wooden bar and ordered a rye. The bartender had a thin, carefully trimmed moustache and his hair was slicked back with some type of grease. He was short and stocky, but his thick arms warned of a wicked punch if necessary.

Thanking the man for the rye, Oli looked around the room. It had the same mix of customers as the other two, but the crowd was a little smaller. In one corner lay a table and chairs broken in an earlier confrontation.

"Looks like you had some trouble here," he said, nodding toward the damaged furniture.

"Yep, sure did," the bartender scowled. "Some damn big bruiser mixed it up with a couple of drifters. I put a knot on the bruiser's head and the others headed for the hills. With them went half my crowd. Mostly soldiers."

Suddenly, the rye lost its appeal. Turning, Oli left the saloon and headed for the hotel. It did not sound like Bart would be in any condition to help him tomorrow. He wondered if any information was learned from his contact at the fort. He felt a slow burn as he turned into the hotel. He figured the big man would be sleeping it off in the room.

Pulling the latchstring, Oli stepped into the room ready to read from the book to Bart. His heart fell when he saw the empty cot.

"Where the hell are you, Bart?" he muttered. Lighting the lamp and setting it to burn low, he sat on the cot and took out the tally book. Carefully, he evaluated his assets. Bart's name was in the column.

"You are no damn asset," he growled, throwing the tally book on the table.

Lying back on the cot, he waited for the big man to get in. He needed to know what Bart had found out. The bartender had mentioned two men. Could they have been the men they were following? "It's unlikely that they were," he said, shaking his head, his words unheard in the empty room.

Pondering the turn of events, Oli dozed off. The days on the road were taking their toll. He was not aware of the group of soldiers assembling at the fort as the sergeant looked over his men. Spitting a stream of tobacco juice, the sergeant wiped his mouth with the back of his hand.

"Now, the word is the man in staying at the Lazy. Nothing was said about the others. We need to take him alive and squeeze him for information." Staring sternly at the men, the sergeant turned. "Let's go get 'im."

The slamming of a door and the shouting of orders brought Oli wide awake. For a moment, he was confused about where he was. The lamp beside the bed was set to burn low and was sending shadows on the canvas walls, which seemed to dance as the breeze outside caused them to flutter. He realized he was lying fully dressed on his bed.

The loud voices were coming closer. He could hear the proprietor complaining, "Please keep your voices down. I have sleeping guests. Follow me, I'll show you where the men you are looking for are."

A glance at the empty cot next to him confirmed that Bart had not returned. In a quick motion, Oli turned the lamp off and scooped up the tally book. Then, reaching under his cot, he grabbed his saddle bags.

The light going off caused the men in the hall to start running. Slipping the Good Knife from its sheath, he slit the canvas wall and slipped into the night. There were loud voices on both sides of him as well as behind. Close to the wall of his room was a drainage ditch. Stumbling into it unexpectedly caused him to fall headlong into the foul smelling water.

Someone fired a shot at the sound. Another hollered as the blind shot came too close. The men outside were in a crossfire situation. Both sides were yelling at each other and Oli took advantage of the noise, crawling swiftly along the ditch to the stone wall.

There was a cedar board opening which allowed the drainage to flow under the thick wall. It was large enough for Oli to crawl into and hide while the men searched for him. Crouching against one side to the planks, he gasped to catch his breath. The water in the ditch was a combination of kitchen and toilet sewage. The smell almost overwhelmed him.

The footsteps of two men came toward his hiding place. With his heart pounding in his ears, Oli prayed that they would not find him. Anger was building as he lay in his putrid hole. This was the second time he had been rousted out of bed by men searching for him. It did not make sense. He decided that if one of the soldiers stuck his head into the culvert, he would take his chances and put a bullet between the man's eyes.

Suddenly, one of the men spoke. "Careful, Wally. Ya don't want to step into that ditch. You'll ruin your boots in that privy water."

"Damn, Tip, you should have warned me sooner. I think I got some of it on my boot. The bloomin' boot will stink for a week."

Chuckling, Wally kidded his companion.

"Since you got the smell on your boot already, you can wade on in and check under the wall."

"The hell you say. If he's laying in that stuff, let him stay. I ain't gonna wrestle him."

"You figure he helped the lieutenant escape?" Tip asked.

"The sergeant thinks he did. The telegram said he had help and they killed a guard."

"I knew the fella they killed," Tip replied. "Believe he had a wife and couple of kids in the east somewhere."

Their voices faded as they walked away from the drainage ditch. *Martin has escaped?* Oli wondered. *A guard killed? It can't be Martin they're talking about.*

Moving as quietly as possible, he continued through the sucking, tepid mud and water. The men were right about one thing. The smell on his clothes and boots would be a long time coming off. The steam bath and laundry was wasted. His saddle bags had hit the filthy water when he fell. Afterward, he had slung them over his shoulder and prevented them from being submerged in the liquid.

Emerging on the far side of the stone wall, Oli climbed out of the ditch. There were some low bushes a short distance from the wall and he headed for them, running in a low crouch. Resting briefly, he squeezed the water out of his wool pants and socks. Holding his boots upside down, water poured out. He was not far from the pole barn where he had his bay. With his soggy boots back on, he moved from one dense shadow to the next, working his way to his horse.

Lying under an oak tree about 30 dangerous

steps from the pole barn, he searched for any movement. Nothing stirred. Taking his time, he crawled towards the barn. The open space between the tree and barn seemed to take forever. Oli was expecting a shot in the back at any time. He dared not move faster for fear that it would catch the attention of a watcher.

Finally reaching the barn wall, he found that he was trembling from the strain. Resting for a moment, he continued to the door. Reaching up, he lifted the metal latch and pulled the door open. The noise of the latch and the squeak of the hinges sounded like thunder in the stillness of the night. Ducking into the barn, he pulled the door shut.

The bay snorted loudly, no doubt at the foul smell he brought into the stable. Waiting just a bit longer, Oli decided that he was finally safe. The horse stepped away from him as he approached. Soft words of assurance settled it down.

"What the hell is that smell!" a voice from the back of the stable growled.

Oli froze with fear for a split-second, then dove into the stall behind the bay. Scrambling to get deeper in the shadows, he slipped and slid in the manure.

"Who's out there and what the hell are you doing with my partner's horse?" the voice demanded.

Realizing what the man had said, Oli recognized the voice. "Is that you, Bart?"

There was the sound of stumbling and bumping as the man staggered toward the bay's stall.

"Some bitching dark barn. A guy could get killed trying to get through here." The huge frame came into view in the dim light. He was leaning against a grain barrel to steady himself.

"Where were you this evening? And did you find out anything at the fort?" Oli demanded.

"I'm sorry, pard. I guess I had a couple drinks after leaving the fort and sort of lost track of time," Bart replied with a bit of a slur.

Coughing and clearing his throat, he continued. "I did find out that there was one deserter. A fellow named Topper. Know him from Fort Leavenworth. He was reported missing the same time as the robbery."

"You didn't see this Topper anywhere here, did you?"

"It's you I smell. Whew, where have you been? I thought you were going to clean up after I left."

"I was chased out of our room by soldiers. I had to escape by way of the drainage ditch. One of the things it drained was the toilet. While hiding under the wall, I overheard a couple of the soldiers say Martin had escaped. Maybe killed someone while doing it."

Rubbing his chin, Oli shook his head. "I don't know why they would be looking for me, or how they would know where I was."

"Aw damn. That might have been my fault. I did run across the man Topper and some other guy, over in the Barrel. I was talking to the bartender about Martin, and about you and me hunting for the stolen payroll to clear him."

"This Topper comes up to me and says, 'What do you know about the lieutenant?'"

"I told him it was none of his damn business.

That was when I recognized him. I tried to grab him and the other guy. We wrestled for a bit and I would have got 'em for you, too, but someone clubbed me from behind. Next thing I knew, I was in the street. There was a full bottle of rye next to me. Drank most of it to stop the ache in my head, and then come here to sleep it off before coming to you with the info."

Oli sat listening to his huge friend in disbelief. He had let the men they needed to find know they were looking for them. They had gotten away. No doubt they had left the bottle, knowing Bart would drink it. And if they knew about Martin's escape, they could have implied that he had helped when tipping off the sergeant about his staying at the hotel.

Bart's hand slipped off the grain barrel and he almost fell. Grabbing the side of the stall was the only thing that stopped him from hitting the floor. "Sorry, Oli, still a bit unsteady. Gimme an hour or so and I will be good as new."

That was the second time Bart had apologized. Oli had never heard the man do that before. The two men had several hours' head start on them and he could not wait for the big man to sober up. Not to mention, he was a hunted man. Sooner or later, the search would cover this building.

His big friend, the man he was depending on helping him in the hunt, was perched in front of him, hardly able to sit on the barrel. It was time to leave him behind.

"Bart, I am going alone. I cannot spend each day wondering if you might run across a bottle of rye." Oli felt hot anger flowing through his veins. He fought to keep it out of his voice. "You were an asset at the start, but now are not." Turning from the big man, he said, "Be well, my friend."

He could not see the brutal expression on Bart's face. To be rebuffed by this little man, combined with the alcohol flowing through his brain, clouded his mind.

Staggering toward the back of the barn, he snarled, "You little pup, you think I need the trouble you brought me? I am tired of having to lead you by the nose all the time." Returning to the back of the barn, he fell heavily into the pile of hay.

Rolling on his back, he hollered, "Besides, you stink!"

Oli knew it was the drink talking, but the words still hurt. He quickly saddled the bay and secured his bedroll and saddlebags. Stowing some extra supplies he had left in the barn, he turned to lead the horse outside. For a moment, he wanted to say something before leaving. The loud snores of the sleeping man came from the back. Another time, he decided, and moved out into the night.

His soggy britches chafed his inner thighs as he walked the horse toward the west. The direction wasn't chosen for any special reason. His gut told him that the running men would not head toward the river. Going south would bring them into contact with the Mexican Army. Most important, he remembered a stream about three miles from the fort that he could use to clean up.

CHAPTER SEVEN

The chorus of frogs and the lonely hoot of an owl were combined with the splashing of Oli in his long johns, sitting in the middle of the stream. His left hand held a large bar of homemade soap and his right his wool pants. On the bushes next to the stream were draped his freshly scrubbed shirt and socks. The cold water helped to take the heat out of his chafed thighs.

The bay, on its picket rope, foraged for the sweet grasses along the bank, its ears twitching as it caught the night sounds. The saddle lay next to a hastily made camp. It and the saddle bags would also get a good cleaning before the night was over.

Oli was tired and dearly wanted to curl up in his bedroll, but the awful smelling clothes and gear had to be dealt with immediately. Some of the smell would remain for some time, but at least he would know they were clean.

Every once in a while, he would sit quietly in the water listening for any sound of pursuit. Evidently there was none. It was possible that the sergeant had taken it upon himself to try and capture Oli. He would have had to wait until morning to do anything more than a local search.

Ringing the excess water out of his britches, he put them next to the other clothes. Then, removing his long johns, he gave them a good rinse. Shivering from the night chill, he tossed the underwear on one of the bushes, hurried back to his camp and wrapped his blanket around his trembling, naked body.

He decided it was safe to make some coffee. Putting together a small pile of twigs and bark, he struck the flint. The shower of sparks was a comforting sight, giving the promise of warmth soon to come. While the pot of water was heating on the small fire, he took his spare clothing from his saddle bags and dressed. The scratchiness of the clean long johns made him think of the Saturday night saunas back in Elkader. He and Joan would sit watching the river, all clean and flushed from their weekly bath.

The coffee was satisfying, warming his insides. He had just finished cleaning his leather gear with saddle soap. Oli was starting to feel human again. He chewed on a piece of hard bread that he'd gotten from Dixie's while staring into the night. Twice, he thought he'd seen a flicker of a campfire. Based on the North Star, the fire was west and a bit north.

Someplace to head for in the morning, he thought. With eyes growing heavy, he pulled his blanket tight around his shoulders and settled his head on the freshly cleaned saddle. His rifle had been in the barn and was clean. He had checked the revolver and other than getting wet, it had no mud in it. He would oil it in the morning. Within moments, he was fast asleep.

The sun was up when he woke. Dew was heavy on the grass, so his clothes would be far from dry. He needed to check out the possible campfire sighting. For a moment, he expected to see Bart walking over from checking on the horses. The memories of the previous night flooded back. He started to second-guess himself. He needed the tracking experience of Bart. Away from the saloons, the big man would have stayed sober.

Too late to go back, he realized. Breakfast was another piece of hard bread and cold coffee left over from the late night pot. He wiped the revolver with an oily rag and reloaded it while eating. The bay stomped impatiently as the blanket and saddle were put into place. With the horse saddled and most of the evidence of his camp wiped out, it was time to go. The damp clothes would have to finish drying at tonight's camp. By the sun, he estimated that it was mid-morning. He should have moved out earlier, but last night's events had left him exhausted.

It was impossible to estimate the distance of the campfire that he thought he had seen. Oli looked the landscape over. There was a bluff on the horizon. Someone could have been spending the night at the base. The clomping of the bay's hooves and the creak of his saddle were the only sounds in the still morning. He wished there was someone to talk to, somebody to help plan the next move.

Rubbing the animal's neck he said, "What do you think about the direction we are going, horse?" It bobbed its head, enjoying the attention of the rider.

"Glad to know you agree with me." After a

few minutes of riding in silence, Oli decided to tell the bay about the good horse he'd gone west with some years back. As he talked to the horse, he searched the horizon for any movement. The bluff was getting closer and was much wider than it looked in the distance. Odds of finding a camp began to feel slim.

It was mid-afternoon when he saw a row of trees that gave promise of water. It seemed to join the base of the bluff in the distance. A shallow creek wound between the rolling plains. Dismounting next to an inviting pool, he let the horse drink. Washing the dust from his face, he looked up and down the creek. There was a chance the camp was along this creek.

Sitting on a rock next to the water, he removed his hat and slowly turned it in his hands. His thoughts were about Martin. If he escaped from the fort, what direction would he be taking? Who would have helped him break out? There had been three men they were following at one time. Could the third man have gone back and helped Martin get away? Maybe the plan was to kill him to end the search for the payroll.

For a moment, Oli felt overwhelmed by the whole situation. His original goal had been to find the money and prove Joan's brother was innocent. Now that a man was killed during the escape, was there any way to prove Martin innocent? Even if the silver and gold was found along with the actual thieves, he would still face a murder charge. He now had no way of evading being hung. Unless he continued to run, his life would be worthless.

A chill went up his spine. The army might think that he was the other man who had helped Martin get away! How could he prove that he was not?

The first night in the hotel, when the soldiers had come looking for him, might have been because of the escape and not the knife incident in the saloon.

The bay nuzzled Oli with its wet nose. It brought him out of deep thought. Birds were singing, the sun was warm on his back. A soft breeze ruffled his hair. Now was not the time to sit here and stew. If ever there was a time he needed to evaluate assets and liabilities, it was now.

Taking the tally book out of his saddle bag, he opened to a blank page. At the top he made a note that as far as supplies went, he was in good shape. The sun slowly moved across the afternoon sky as he listed the options and problems posed with each one. Looking over his notes, choices began to develop. Several were discarded and scratched out. He looked at the remaining three.

There was no benefit to finding Martin. Unless he was recaptured, there was no danger of being hung. If they were found together, he would be implicated in the jail break and murder. Joan's brother's fate was cast. He needed to be left alone to disappear.

If he was able to find the gold, there was a chance that returning it would prove that he was not involved with the escape. Also, the actual robbers would pay for the crime.

A third option was to find Bart and convince him to go back to Fort Leavenworth to vouch for his innocence in the escape. That, is, if Bart's word still held any weight back at the fort. He could then be done with the problem and head for home.

Leaning heavily toward the third option, Oli began to make a small fire and heat water for coffee.

His damp and slightly smelly clothes were back on some bushes to finish drying. First, he needed to return to Fort Scott and track down Bart.

Loosening the cinch on the bay, he put it on a picket rope to crop some grass. Right now he was no more than a half-day's ride from Fort Scott. After a bit to eat and a little rest, he could ride back and find Bart. Arriving after dark would be an advantage. He could wait for him at the pole barn.

The strong coffee and thick strips of fried bacon seemed like a meal fit for a king. The tension Oli had been under the past couple of weeks was gone. His brother-in-law was no longer his problem. It was early June and he would be home in time to put in a few vegetables and well in advance of the birth of his second child.

Soaking a piece of hard bread in the bacon grease, he anticipated enjoying it once it was sufficiently softened. A fish jumped in the slow-moving pool of the creek. *I should have tried for some fresh fish for my meal,* he thought, smiling at the idea of how good they would have tasted.

Pouring another cup of coffee, he set it down to let it cool just a bit while he moved the bay's picket. He noticed that the horse was watching something in the distance. Looking over, Oli could see what looked like a dust devil about a mile away. At second glance, he realized it was a half-dozen riders. It appeared they were on his back trail. He observed them stopping for a moment as a man got down off his horse and checked the ground. He waved and pointed along the trail Oli had ridden.

They were soldiers! And they were following

him. By now they were just over a half-mile away and he could hear one of them shouting and motioning in his direction. They had spotted him!

Grabbing his coffee pot and saddlebags, he hurriedly put them on the bay. Then, tightening the cinch and pulling the picket loose, he rushed to mount the horse. Startled, it stepped away from him, causing his foot to miss the stirrup. He fell heavily against the animal and grabbed the saddle horn to stop from falling. For just a moment, the animal and man dance around until Oli finally swung up into the saddle.

The soldiers were riding full out after him. He was thankful that the bay had drunk and eaten, with time to rest. He was sure it could quickly carry him away from his pursuers. Not knowing what direction would be best to run, he crossed the creek and headed north toward the rolling plains. On the grasslands there was no place to hide, so he had to depend on the horse outlasting theirs.

With the bay at a gallop and bending low in the saddle, Oli rode like the devil himself was after him. The horse was fresh and eager to run. Soon, the soldiers' shouts disappeared and the only sound was the steady rhythm of his horse's hooves and its heavy breathing. He tried to keep to the lower areas.

Forced to ride over a ridge, he looked back to see how far the soldiers were behind him. They were out of sight, behind a rise. There was no doubt that they would keep on coming. He slowed the bay to give it a breather and continued down the other side of the ridge. In front of him was another line of trees with a shallow river running through them.

Putting the horse into the water, he let it walk

east, hoping that the soldiers would expect him to continue moving west. The sun was getting low in the western sky and darkness was about an hour away. He shuddered to think about another long night with little sleep.

With the immediate threat of being overtaken gone, Oli began to take a mental inventory. It helped knowing what his strengths were. He considered the three plans he had come up with. Going to find Bart was now out of the question. The risk was too high. He would have to try and find the men's trail and bring them back to justice with the gold. This scenario was much more difficult than the first one he had chosen.

He was well supplied for the hunt . . . or was he? He'd left the spare clothes behind! Well, the clothes he was wearing were in good repair and should be adequate. Reaching back to feel for his fry pan and coffee pot brought more bad news. The grease-covered pan was there, but the coffee pot was gone! Dropped, maybe, when he was trying to get mounted, or shaken loose during the gallop.

He let the bay pick its way along the river. There was a feeling of relief when the sun went down and they traveled in a cloak of darkness. Oli's eyes burned from the lack of sleep. The walking horse rocked him with a hypnotic motion. He closed his eyes to relieve the burning. Slumped in the saddle, the dark figure of a man and horse moved ever so slowly along the river.

The lack of movement woke Oli. He had no idea where he was, but for some reason the horse had stopped. It stood spread-legged, with its head hanging low. The area around him gradually came into focus.

The horse was standing just outside the water. The river was now flowing from the north, so sometime in the night the course had changed. By the stars, it was well after midnight.

He felt a twinge of guilt, realizing that the horse had been carrying its burden for well over four hours. Dismounting, he felt stiff and sore. With difficulty, he stooped and took a drink from the river and then walked the horse up the bank to a grassy area. Removing the saddle and bridle, he rubbed it down with hands full of grass. Once on the picket rope, the bay enjoyed a good roll.

Still too tired to set up a proper camp, he laid on the grass, using the saddle for a pillow and covered himself with a blanket. Nature's call woke him about an hour before sunrise. As he finished up, a sound caught his attention. There was grunting and snorting coming from out on the plain. The sound seemed to be coming from a wide area.

Pulling the blanket around his shoulders, he sat staring toward the sounds, waiting for the morning light to reveal the source. Finally, he could make out shadowy hulks moving slowly across the grasslands. Soon, he was able to see the large herd of buffalo. He could see the steam rising from their massive bodies in the morning chill.

Oli was fearful of drawing attention with a fire, so he filled his cup with water from the river and chewed on his last piece of hard bread. As he ate, his stomach ached with hunger. It had been late afternoon the day before when he had last eaten.

The bay stared at the buffalo and appeared ready to face a day of traveling. Suddenly, Oli had an idea. It was only a matter of time before the soldiers would find his tracks leaving the water. If he rode amongst the buffalo, they would wipe out any sign of his trail and they wouldn't know what direction he'd taken. Quickly, he struck his crude camp and saddled the horse.

Rubbing its forehead, he talked the plan over with the animal. "I want you to ride into the gaps of the buffalo. They are strung out for over a mile and heading west. We can stay in front of them and let their hooves churn our tracks to dust." The bay rubbed its head against him as though it understood. In reality, it liked having its forehead scratched.

A line of thunderheads were building in the west as Oli rode toward an opening in the buffalo herd. As he approached the curly-haired beasts, they took little notice of him. What they saw was a four-legged animal walking among them and had little fear due to their enormous size. Once, when they rode too close to a young bull, it snorted and challenged them.

The Hawken rifle lay across the saddle in front of him. In case one of the more aggressive bulls came at them, he would be able to shoot and stop the attack. The herd was drifting northwest, toward a rise in the plains. The river he had left could still be seen behind him. Stopping for a minute to drink from his canteen, Oli thought he saw a flash of light toward the river.

Swinging down from the bay, he stood watching for any movement. About a mile away, he caught sight of riders. They were working their way along the river. It could only be the soldiers searching for the point where he had left the river. He was well into the herd of buffalo and it was unlikely that they had seen him.

Dismounting and walking alongside the horse, he continued over the rise. He caught sight of the bluff he had ridden toward the day before. He planned to swing around and see if he could cut the trail of the two men he was looking for.

Safely out of sight of the soldiers, he mounted and trotted the bay along the route of the buffalo to put more distance between himself and his pursuers. His thoughts were on those behind him and he did not see the riders sweeping down from an opposing ridge. A dozen young Kickapoo braves rode hard toward the buffalo. Their cries caught his attention, giving him chills of pending danger. A large group from the herd broke into a run, sending up a cloud of dust and the thunder of hooves.

Oli wheeled the bay and rode hard toward the edge of the herd to get clear of the charging animals. Looking quickly over his shoulder, he realized that the braves were focused on the buffalo and may not have noticed him. Crouching low on the bay, he broke out of the herd and put some distance between himself and the Indians. There was no way for him to know that the Kickapoo were not a danger to the whites.

Being on the safe side of the stampeding herd, he pulled up and dismounted. Kneeling on the ground, he readied the Hawken for fear that the braves would break from the herd and come his way. He was fascinated to watch the braves ride among the stampeding buffalo and shoot deadly arrows into the beasts.

Without warning, one of the wounded bulls charged the hunter. It struck the horse, knocking it down, throwing its rider. The young man rolled as he hit the ground, coming back to his feet, and then ran away from the angry bull. The other braves broke away from the herd to go after the fallen comrade. Within seconds, the bull would be on the Indian. Without hesitation, Oli lifted the Hawken and took aim at the animal. Squeezing off the shot, the bull faltered and collapsed just steps short of the fleeing brave.

The crash of the rifle caused the Indians to pull up. Seeing the yellow-haired man for the first time, they began to slowly circle Oli. The exhausted brave stood with his hands on his knees, looking at the man who had saved him from a certain death.

With the Hawken empty, Oli felt vulnerable to attack. He had the revolver on his hip. Its effective range would put the Indians too close before he could start firing. The brave he had saved shouted something. The other Kickapoo stopped the circling action and moved to the standing Indian. It was apparent that this man was their leader. The leader raised his hand in salute to Oli.

Relieved, he mounted the bay. The startled buffalo had moved out of range of any more hunting. Raising his hand in response to the leader's gesture, he guided the bay away from the braves and the half-dozen buffalo that lay dying on the grassy plains in the wake of the Kickapoos' efforts.

Oli did not look back as he rode away, but rather he sat as tall as his short stature would allow. It felt good to know that he had saved a man's life. In front of him the grassy plain rose on both sides. He was riding into a valley somewhere in Kansas, without a clue of what the future would bring. For the moment he did not care, he felt good.

CHAPTER EIGHT

The smell of rain was in the air as Oli set up his evening camp. He had found a grove of aspen near a swampy area. Darkness would come early due to the heavy, angry-looking clouds. Gusts of warm, humid wind rustled the leaves. The sound was comforting. Before starting supper, he spread his rain slicker over the blanket. If the storm broke before the meal was done, at least his bed would be dry.

Lightning began to flash, followed by crashes of thunder. The wind was becoming stronger, making it impossible to get a fire going. The bay was standing with its head up, nervously watching the storm. Oli realized that he had chosen a poor location to spend the night. If the rain was severe, the area could be flooded around him. There was a dry stream bed that led to the swamp, right beside his camp. It could become a raging torrent before this blew over.

With his saddle and gear back on the horse, Oli led the animal through the trees. He was in a dilemma.

The trees were the highest point on the plains and could draw lightning. But once they were out of the trees, he and the horse became a high point.

All of a sudden, he was struck on the back by something. At the same time, the bay began to squeal and pull on the reins. All around them hailstones were falling. Some were as large as small potatoes. When hitting the ground they would bounce back into the air. He fought to control the horse. Several hail stones struck the two with a force that would leave bruises.

As quickly as the hail came, it stopped and a rain, driven horizontal by the wind, came in a downpour. The wind was whipping his slicker, making it all but useless to keep him dry. The horse stood on trembling legs as the wind, rain, and lightning surrounded them.

They had moved halfway up the rise and could overlook the aspen grove and swamp. The trees were thrashing back and forth. All at once the clouds seemed to come down from the sky in a long, dark, whirling arm, as a tornado tore at the grass, throwing the vegetation into the air. The whirling arm went through the aspen grove and the trees were pulled up by their roots and toppled. The water in the swamp seemed to be sucked up into the cloud.

The roar was deafening. Oli wrapped his blanket over the terrified horse's head and forced it to the ground. Debris and rain blinded him as it swirled around, hitting them from all directions. Oli laid on top of the horse and prayed like he had never prayed before. This was surely hell on earth.

He stayed there with the bay as the thunderous sound moved away. They were covered with grass and dirt. The wind died down some and a cool, cleansing rain began to fall. Sitting back with the reins firmly clenched in his hand, he let the horse stand up. It stood with head hanging, exhausted from the terrifying experience.

Oli became aware that his rain slicker was gone, ripped from his body. His hat was a mangled mess, saved only because of the leather string under his chin. His neck was chafed from the tugging action of the hat in the wind. He was astounded that he had not noticed either the slicker or the hat during the storm.

Standing and rubbing the bay's neck, he said. "I am not sure what they call it our here, but I have heard of cyclones or whirlwinds. You know what, horse? I think we have just seen one up close."

Shaking his head, he added, "Too damn close."

His clothes and blanket were soaked and mud-covered. The wind had mostly died down and the rain had stopped momentarily. "I think we need to go back to the aspens and get a fire going."

There was not much daylight left as they walked toward the aspen grove. Shocked, Oli looked at what had been a healthy grove of trees, now nothing but splintered limbs and tree trunks. Roots were pulled from the ground. Little was left standing. He realized that had he stayed near the stream, they would have been pulled into the angry arm and more than likely killed. He took a moment to thank Providence for guiding him out of the grove before the storm.

Supper was a slow affair. First, he made coffee using the fry pan. Then, after drinking all but the last cupful, he used it to fry bacon and a bit of sourdough. He huddled close to the fire while he ate. The soggy clothing offered little warmth against the now cool evening.

After eating, he brushed the horse, as much for the warmth of the animal's body as for its need for attention. The task was accomplished in his long johns while his clothes were draped over sticks next to the fire. The whirlwind had provided plenty of wood for a good fire. The only dry item he had was the saddle blanket. The saddle had offered some protection from the storm. He would use this as a blanket tonight.

The sky was clear and the sun bright in the morning. Oli sat on the ground tarp, absorbing the warming rays. He surveyed the devastation that surrounded them. It was a sight he would never forget. The path of the storm leaving the grove was littered with pieces of the aspens. The grass had a trampled look, having been torn at by the severe winds.

While they were far from clean, his clothes were acceptably dry. The bay was grazing peacefully, as though nothing had happened the night before. He envied the animals. While frightened by the action of storms, as soon as it was over birds were singing and others were going about their business, the danger forgotten.

Mid-morning brought them far from the destroyed aspen grove. The paint brush was in bloom across the grass land, clusters of blue or yellow flowers dotting the plain. A killdeer ran in front of the bay, dragging a wing as though injured. Once it thought that the man and horse were drawn far enough from the nest, it flew away.

On the horizon, he could see something white, or an off-white on the ground. There seemed to be several of them. *Maybe a scattering of boulders,* he thought. As he drew closer the skinned carcasses of buffalo were revealed. The breeze brought the smell of rotting meat well before he got close to the slaughtered animals.

The bay stepped anxiously, not liking the odor. He guided it around the carnage. Oli estimated that there were 30 kills, a good day's work for the hunters. Even though he was some distance away, the sound of buzzing flies could be heard. A shadowy figure caught his eye, moving around the remains. A second look brought the wolf into focus.

"Good day Mister Wolf. Today I have enough to eat, so you go about enjoying your meal," he told the sly animal. On his first trip into the wilderness, he'd had to eat the wolves that were following him to stay alive. It was that, or be eaten himself once he'd become too weak.

While taking a rest to eat a midday meal, he noticed something moving slowly across the plain. At first he thought it was a couple of buffalo, but as it got a bit closer he could see that it was a wagon pulled by two horses. It was headed in his direction. After eating, he decided to take a course that would intercept the traveler.

It was late afternoon when Oli drew near. The wagon had stopped and two men were setting up camp. One man was large, with a scruffy, black beard. The other was smaller, with sandy colored hair. Both wore buckskin clothing with low-heeled boots.

The smell of the hide wagon reached him before he got to the camp. The men's clothing was dirty and stained with blood and animal fat. The big

111

man had a cheek full of chew and spat as Oli approached.

"Hello, the camp," he said. "My name is Oli August."

The sandy-haired man was not much more than a boy. He gave a quick smile. "I'm Ernie, and this is my cousin, Alvin. Have a set, we was just about to make some viddles."

"Thank you, I will," Oli replied. He kept his eyes on the big man. He didn't seem to have anything to say, but stared intently at the bay.

Swinging down, he offered to contribute and help with the meal. Ernie smiled and shook his head. "No need, Mister August. I'm a pretty fair hand with the cooking and we got us some prime buffalo tongue. Put up your horse and bring your plate and cup."

The big man walked by Oli as he loosened the cinch and picketed the bay so it could graze a spell. "Nice horse you got there, Mista August," he said, followed by a big sluice of tobacco juice.

Watching Alvin walk away, he felt the hair on his neck stand on end. In an unconscious motion, he checked his revolver and knife at his sides and the Good Knife at the nape of his neck.

Ernie was right. He was quite the cook around the campfire. With the coffee done first, he poured the stout brew into Oli's cup. A large black skillet held the buffalo meat. He was frying them with wild onions. A Dutch oven held some nicely browned biscuits. Another pot was warming beans cooked for an earlier meal.

To have so many pots, Oli thought. He was

thankful that the fire was located upwind from the hide wagon. The smell of the ripe hides would have most surely ruined his appetite.

In no time, they were digging into heaping plates of meat and beans. The biscuits were used to sop up the juices from the plates. It was all washed down with more coffee.

"You're a fine cook, Ernie," Oli complimented the young man.

"He's just showin' off fer company," the big man snorted, ladling some more beans onto his plate.

"Am not," Ernie replied to Alvin. Turning to Oli, he continued. "Most often we ain't got time to make a good meal. We got skinnin' and fleshin' the hides to do. We eat quick and simple. Today we saw you comin' our way, so I told Alvin it's time for a big meal."

"For that I thank you. I have been in search of a couple of men traveling in this area. Might be three of them now. I am not sure what they look like. I would recognize the horse tracks."

For the first time, Ernie frowned. "Two days ago, we had a couple of men ridin' double come into camp. Offered them some supper and told them one could ride in the wagon till we got to a town. Alvin here had a good-looking dun. He used the horse to go scouting for buffalo. The two men . . . ah, one's name was Tupper or somethin' like that, the other, I don't remember."

"One of the men I am looking for is named Topper," Oli replied.

"That's it, "Ernie said. "Anyway, just after

eatin', the weather started to kick up. Alvin here was busy preventing our tent from blowin' away." He stabbed at the fire with a stick before continuing. "The two of them headed for the horses. It was a bit and they hadn't come back. It was then I noticed their gear was gone. We soon found out, so was the dun."

"You didn't go after them?"

"Stormed most of the night, awful storm. Was next mornin' before we could go look. Any tracks they left was gone. We didn't know which way to go look." Ernie gave a worried look at his cousin, and then said to Oli, "He was killing mad. He ain't been his self since."

"I am going to look for the men. If I find the dun, is there someplace I can leave it for you?"

"We plan to go to the Westport landin'," Ernie said. "It is near where the Kaw and Missouri Rivers meet. Be out of your way, though."

"I will try and send word to the landing if I find it. More than likely, I will be leaving it at Fort Leavenworth."

Alvin looked up and tossed his plate next to the fire. "Them men spoke of Fort Leavenworth. Said they was meeting someone from there." Anger blazed in his eyes. "Wouldn't be you're the one they was looking for?" Grunting, he walked away without waiting for an answer.

"I told you, Mister August, he ain't been the same since. Damn awful touchy now."

"I am sorry for your troubles, Ernie. I thank you again for an excellent meal. I have to leave now and try and catch up with the men. They were involved

114

in a robbery and killing. My brother-in-law was blamed. Once I find them, I will bring them to justice."

Ernie picked up Alvin's plate. "It was good to have a visitor. Like I said, my cousin hasn't been good company to travel with since the horse was took."

Leaving Ernie to clean up the camp, Oli headed for the bay. Standing near his horse was Alvin. Putting the horse between himself and the big man, he stowed his plate and cup in the saddlebags.

"I want the horse," Alvin stated.

"I need this horse to find the men that stole yours."

Stepping back, the big man pulled his skinning knife. "You ain't leaving with this horse."

Feeling a mixture of anger and fear Oli replied, "You don't know me. I can kill you with my knife before you take a step. Ernie needs your help on the hunt. Don't make me kill you."

"Alvin's right, we need your horse," a voice from behind said. "I got a Hawken aimed at your back. Drop the revolver and step away from the bay."

He was trapped. They had drawn him in with a meal with plans to steal his horse.

"I can find the men that took the dun and return it to you."

"We need a horse to hunt buffalo. These plugs pulling our wagon are only good for that and pullin' skin off buffalo. Alvin needs to find the next herd while I move the wagon."

For a long moment, Oli weighed his options. He could draw the Good Knife and possibly kill Alvin. Seconds later, he would be dead from a bullet in the back.

Indicating the knife on his hip and the revolver, Alvin said, "Drop the weapons and step away from the horse."

No doubt they would have to kill him, but they didn't want to take a chance on wounding the bay. The thought was not much consolation.

Oli lifted the revolver from the holster and dropped it into the dirt. Next, he slowly lifted the knife from his left hip.

"Watch how you handle the knife, Mista August," Alvin warned.

Tossing the knife onto the ground, Oli could hear Ernie's footsteps moving to his right. With no other options left, he ducked under the bay's neck. A shot rang out from the Hawken .54 caliber. Ernie's concern about hitting the horse caused the shot to go wide and missed. Now Oli stood within a few steps of Alvin. Thinking he was unarmed, the big man stepped towards Oli with a fiendish smile. The intention was to finish him off with his skinning knife.

Oli's hand grabbed the Good Knife from the nape of his neck and sent it deep into the chest of Alvin. Shocked, the big man's eyes went wide as he clawed at the knife handle protruding from his chest. His knees buckled as he collapsed to his side.

Wasting no time, Oli dove for his revolver. Grabbing it, he rolled away from the bay for a clear shot. He looked up at Ernie, standing with his mouth wide open and the empty Hawken rifle hanging from his right hand. Dropping it, he ran toward his cousin.

"Alvin, Alvin! What did you do to him!" he

shouted as he knelt at the side of the dead man. Oli walked up and pulled the knife from the big man's chest. Ernie cradled Alvin's lifeless head in his lap.

Slipping the revolver and hunting knife into his belt and then wiping the Good Knife on the grass, Oli moved back to the bay. Tightening the cinch, he swung into the saddle.

"Bury your cousin and then head for home, son. You were done wrong by the two men and tried to correct it with another wrong. I am sorry about Alvin. I told him I didn't want to kill him. You shot at me and he came at me with the knife."

Turning the bay away from the camp, he paused a moment. "I will still bring the dun in should I find it."

What was showing on Oli's face and what he was feeling inside were two different things. The calm matter-of-fact advice he was giving Ernie was one thing. Inside, he felt sick. He had now killed two men on the trip to save Joan's brother. Was it becoming easier to kill? He hoped that it wasn't.

Not trusting Ernie, he urged the bay into a trot to put distance between them. The young man could reload the rifle and hit him with a killing shot a quarter-mile away. Their wagon tracks were visible on the grassy plain. Oli decide to follow them to the spot where the buffalo hunters had had their horse stolen.

With the sun going down, he finally felt that he'd put enough distance between the confrontation and himself. Just the same, he took care choosing a campsite. A knoll had been undercut by rubbing buffalo, providing cover on three sides. Supper had been provided by the buffalo hunters, and while coffee would have been desirable, he didn't want to light a fire.

Curling up in his blanket, the sounds of crickets and the wail of coyotes lulled him to sleep. The snorting of the bay woke Oli with a start. His dreams had been more like a nightmare, with something chasing him. He reached for the Paterson Colt and held it under the blanket while carefully searching the area within view. The aroma of a polecat reached his nostrils and set his mind at ease.

Sitting up, he caught sight of the animal waddling away with the horse staring intently at it. The eastern sky was bright red. A light haze and heavy dew on the grass gave warning of a slow warmup. With his blanket wrapped around his shoulders, he drank some water and chewed on a piece of jerky. There was no wood in the area, so Oli decided to collect buffalo chips, or any sticks he passed during the morning travel, and stop for a hot midday meal.

To ward off the morning chill, he had left his wool coat out of the bedroll. Donning it, he saddled the bay. He made a mental promise of giving the horse a good rubdown this evening. Last night's mood didn't leave him with motivation to do anything more than necessary.

The wheel tracks were plain in the morning light. He let the bay choose its own pace as they rode west following the trail. Bobbing its head, the horse was anxious to travel. At one point, Oli came across an area of high ground where the wagon had stopped and the men had spent time looking around, probably hoping to catch sight of the horse thieves. The droppings from their team indicated that it might have been for a while. An hour later, he came to the place where they had weathered the storm.

Oli looked at the campsite with the knowledge he'd acquired from Bart. After carefully walking around the perimeter, he noted any debris. An empty rye bottle had been tossed a short distance from the fire. A cigar stub lay just outside the fire ring, the result of a careless toss. These two items he attributed to the men he was looking for.

Taking down a bundle of buffalo droppings he had collected during the morning, he made up a small fire and put a pan of water to heat. *I should have taken one of Ernie's pots,* he lamented. Shortly, he was drinking a satisfying cup of coffee. While he sipped, he studied the surrounding area. There was an advantage he had over the buffalo hunters. By knowing the direction the men had come from, he could predict where they would go.

Filling his cup with the remaining liquid, Oli whipped the coffee grounds out with a handful of grass before pouring more water into the pan with some beans. Adding wild onions, salt, and a portion of molasses, he sat back. There was a patch of flaming orange paint brush. Two large yellow and black butterflies fluttered from flower to flower. The serenity of the setting was helpful, relieving the ugliness of the killing the day before.

With a belly full of boiled beans, Oli mounted the bay and rode out about two miles. The night the horses were stolen, there had been a severe storm. Nobody would have ridden far in that weather. Once the rain was over, the sign of their trail would remain. He doubted that Ernie or Alvin had searched very far.

Taking a moment to survey, the horizon revealed some higher ground just a bit southwest of his location. He decided to circle to the south first to try and cut a trail.

After two hours of riding south, he did not find any trail. Disappointed, he rode a couple more miles out from the buffalo hunters' camp. Circling back toward the north, Oli painstakingly searched the ground for any trail. At mid-afternoon he crossed a babbling brook. Allowing the horse to drink its fill, he drank and refilled the canteen just upstream. He noticed a slowly moving pool with the promise of fish a short distance away. Loosening the cinch, he picketed the bay on a clover patch. Rigging a pole, he sat next to the pool and soon had several fish.

Daydreaming and waiting for another hungry fish to find the grasshopper on his hook, he noticed a dark patch on the other side. Mild interest soon turned into excited curiosity. The dark patch was out of place. Dropping his pole, Oli waded across the pond. The dark patch was droppings from a horse! A quick look around revealed the tracks of two horses. A short distance further upstream, he saw where they had been watered. He looked over the tracks left by the men. He could not confirm that he had seen them before. Regardless, he was sure that he had found the two he had been looking for.

The tracks were less than two-days old. If the good weather held, he should be able to catch up to them. Returning to the other side of the stream, he picked up his fish and set about making a meal. Cutting some green willow branches, he skewered the cleaned fish and staked them over his fire. The fry pan was warming water for his coffee. He then moved the bay to new grazing.

With the meal finished and a couple of fish wrapped up for later, he secured his gear and took up the trail of the two men. He still had three hours of daylight. By sundown he would know how fast the men were traveling, and a better idea of the direction.

He pondered where the payroll might be. When he and Bart had been following the men, they had found evidence of a place where it might have been buried for safety. These men had no packhorse. At one time, they had been riding double. Had the money been split up? There had been a third person earlier. Maybe he had it. If that was the case, these two would be riding to a meeting place.

The men he was tracking made no effort to hide their trail. They were riding easily and stopped often. Excitement began to build in Oli. If they kept up this pace, he should be able to come up on them sometime tomorrow. He kept riding until there wasn't enough daylight to see the men's tracks.

He was out on open ground. It was too late to ride and find a protected campsite. While pulling the saddle from the bay, he remembered his mental promise to give the horse a good rubdown. His muscles were stiff and sore from the long day's ride. All he wanted to do was spread his blanket and turn in. Taking the brush from his saddlebag, he walked to the picketed bay. It stood with its head high, knowing what was coming. As Oli brushed the horse, it shook its head and snorted.

A chilling wind was blowing across the plains when he finally crawled under his blanket. He spread his coat on top of the blanket for additional warmth.

He thought about the weather being unusually cool for the time of year. The crunching sound of the happy bay cropping grass was the last sound he remembered as sleep overtook him.

Oli dreamt of home. Joan was baking an apple pie. His son Karl was playing near the hot stove and he kept warning him to be careful. Suddenly, Karl, tripped and fell toward the stove. Oli woke up shouting, "No!"

It was still dark and the chilling wind was blowing through the blanket. He groped around for his coat. Spreading it back over the blanket, he curled in a ball, pulling his knees up. His feet hurt with cold. *What I wouldn't do to be able to put them near the hot stove in my dream,* he thought.

The cold allowed very little sleep for the rest of the night. Getting dressed at first light, he shivered and looked around for anything to make a fire. Nothing! When he left the stream, he was in a hurry. Following the trail had consumed him the day before and he hadn't collected anything to burn. If the wind would only stop blowing, he knew he could warm up.

While saddling the bay, he wrapped his arms around the horse to gain some of its warmth. He remembered doing this as a boy back in Finland when they went to milk on cold winter mornings. Swinging up into the saddle, he wore his wool coat for protection against blustery weather.

It had been dark when he had finally stopped the night before. The trail had been lost a short time before stopping. It took a few minutes of cutting back and forth to pick it up. He turned to follow the tracks, the cold air blowing in his face. Turning his collar up and pulling his hat brim down to protect his face, he shivered.

"Well, horse, why does the trail have to lead into the wind?" he said, rubbing the animal's neck as he urged it forward.

CHAPTER NINE

After an hour on the trail, Oli reached inside his coat and brought out the two,remaining fish. His own body heat had taken the chill off them. With cold and stiff fingers, he plucked the tender meat from the bones. Finishing the fish, he took a long drink of water. It wasn't much of a breakfast, but it prevented any delay getting started.

The trail continued to be easy to follow. The hills he had seen the day before seemed to be the destination for the riders. As Oli rode, he kept an eye out for material to build a fire with. He had found a good supply of buffalo chips. These he was putting into a flour sack tied to his saddle horn. The sun slowly climbed up the morning sky. Despite the wind, the heat of the sun soon won out and the coat was taken off and tied to the back of the saddle.

Wanting to let the bay rest for awhile, he made coffee and chewed on the last of his jerky. It was evident that hunting to supplement his supplies was necessary. He had three, maybe four days of food left if he ate sparingly. Water was not a problem. This time of year rain had left all the lakes, ponds, and swamps filled. The smaller streams were still flowing. Later in the summer, many of these would dry up.

The hills he was heading toward were now about less than a day's ride away. They would be reached by nightfall. He would be exposed for some distance before getting there. Oli's plan was to stop about an hour away from them and wait for darkness. He would then close in on the hills and spend the night. If he saw any fire, he would stay clear tonight and check it out early in the morning.

What he expected to find, or even say to the men once he caught up to them, he was not sure of. They'd had a fight with Bart over Martin. They might attack him, or possibly run. He reached into his saddlebag and took out the spare cylinder for the Paterson Colt. His older model had not been updated with the loading lever, so he carried the extra to extend his firepower. The loading lever would allow the rider to reload while on horseback. Without it, he'd have to stop.

Just before kicking dust over his fire, he saw movement a dozen yards beyond the horse. Taking time, he carefully searched the area. Again, he saw movement. It was a rabbit.

"No time like the present to start adding to the larder," he said under his breath.

Watching until the animal moved away from the bay, he drew the revolver from the holster. From behind him came a nerve-racking screech. Startled, he looked up in time to see a hawk swoop down and pounce on the unsuspecting rabbit. After a short struggle, the steel-like grasp of the hawk's talons took the fight out of the animal. Staring in surprise, Oli stood motionless. Flapping its wings feverishly, the hawk lifted the limp body of the rabbit into the air and headed for its nest of young ones somewhere out on the plain.

Slipping the revolver back into his holster, Oli looked at the bay. "Horse, the hawk got this one, the next one will be mine." Smiling, he began to gather up and stow his gear.

He rode down into a wildflower-covered valley that led to the hills. Oli felt confident that his plan was a good one. Whether the men ahead had the payroll or not, he was sure that they could at least clear Martin of the robbery and murder of the guard.

The muffled sound of the bay's hooves on the grass was the only sound in the bright afternoon. Oli noticed something dark moving across the valley in front of him. His first guess was a lone buffalo. As he drew closer, he realized that it was too narrow to be a buffalo. It had to be a horse.

He swung down from the bay and walked along, leading it to keep his profile smaller. No horse would be wandering in this country without an owner looking for it. The horse was dragging a picket rope. He stopped a distance away from the animal and scanned the valley beyond it.

After several minutes of watching the horse's back trail, he decided that nobody was following it. By this time the horse was less than a quarter-mile away and was standing looking at them. It was nervous, acting like it might run. Oli stepped to the blind side of the bay and moved toward the animal. His horse whinnied at the loose horse. They were only paces apart. It was a dun. No doubt the buffalo hunter's horse. There was blood on the hind quarters of the horse.

He stepped around the bay and spoke softly to the dun. "What are you doing alone out here? Where are your owners? You stand still and I will take you back." What he said didn't matter to the animal, but his soft tone was what the dun would respond to. Continuing to talk and move closer, the horse reached out its head as Oli took the picket rope.

A quick inspection told him that the blood on the horse was from something other than the dun. He looked at the hills and wondered what had happened up there. They were still a good two hours away. The sun was low in the west. It would be dark in another hour.

Oli knew that he had to follow the dun's trail. Once it was dark he would have to stop. He decided to backtrack the horse until sunset, before making camp. He would still be an hour from the hills. If he saw a fire, he would move in. If not, he would wait until sunrise to continue following the horse's trail. Somewhere, he knew there was a man, wounded or dead.

The horse's trail wandered, typical of a grazing animal. Sundown left him two hours' ride from the hills. Once again, he made a cold camp. Supper consisted of hard bread and water. He chewed slowly, savoring every bite. As dusk settled on the plains, he watched the hills. He hoped that a cook fire would be sighted, so the chase could be over. With luck he could head back toward Fort Leavenworth in the morning, bringing proof that Martin was not involved.

The night sky was clear and a chilling wind began to blow. He watched the dun grazing calmly next to his horse. "What violent thing happened on your back trail?" he asked. Smiling, he muttered, "I guess you ain't talking."

Wrapping the blanket around his shoulders, he lay on his side, head on the saddle, as he watched for any flickering light. Oli was soon sleeping. At some point the horses began to snort and he woke, remaining perfectly still as he watched the darkness. The horses settled down. Oli figured it must have been a wolf or coyote wandering by. He got up to relieve himself before climbing back into his blankets. Settling back down, a worrisome thought entered his mind: *It could be Indians.*

The cold, and thoughts of Indians, kept him sleeping light. The sun was just breaking the horizon and Oli sat with coffee boiling in the fry pan. He kept the fire small and sat close to catch a little of its heat. After the coffee, he put a generous portion of bacon into the pan. He mixed up some corn meal in his coffee mug and fried it in the bacon grease.

Wrapping some of the leftovers in a rag, he packed it into his saddlebag for a later meal. He saddled the dun, giving his bay a rest, and headed out following the trail. It took a few minutes to pick it up. The bay tried to move ahead of the dun. It was evident that it wanted to be the leader. Oli pulled it back and spoke sternly. After a bit of confusion, they were once again following yesterday's tracks.

The morning chill soon turned to a hot and

humid day. The haze burned off and soft breezes from the south brought the moist air. As the dun plodded along, sweat was heavy on Oli's brow and trickling down his back.

Looking around, he scoffed, "Strange weather. I'm freezing one moment, and sweating the next."

He removed his wool shirt and tied it with his coat to the back of the saddle. The Good Knife and sheath went into his saddle bag. He unbuttoned the front of his long john top to take advantage of any gusts on his chest.

The lush, green grass was steadily getting thinner as he started to climb the lower part of the hills. Wiping the sweat from his brow with his neckerchief, he stopped the horses and sat for a moment looking for any sign of movement or a campsite. The hills were sparsely covered with brush and trees. It offered ample hiding for anyone who wanted to ambush a rider.

As he watched, he took the leftover fried cornmeal from his saddle bags and munched on it. Washing the greasy chunks of meal down with water from the canteen completed his midday meal. As he started the dun forward, he took the loop off the Paterson Colt. He then located the spare cylinder in the saddle bags and left it at the top for quick accessibility. Taking the Hawken rifle out of the scabbard, Oli carried it across the saddle. He was still several hundred yards from the first trees. If return fire was needed, it would have to be the rifle.

He gradually began to make out something dark in the wild flowers, just outside of the trees. He stopped the horses and swung down. Taking his time, he looked the area over. Nothing but the dark shape was out of place. Leading the horses, he watched the trees as he headed toward whatever was lying on the ground. Finally, he was able to see that it was a shoulder and arm of a man.

The birds flew from branch to branch. The undisturbed wildlife gave him some assurance that nobody was hiding ahead. Tying the horses to a low bush, he walked up to inspect the man. He was met with the buzzing of flies. Marks on the face were evidence that something had chewed on the body. An ugly wound on the lower back had no doubt been the source of blood on the dun. Closer inspection revealed another wound entering the back of the head and exiting under the jaw, tearing a large hole.

Oli shuddered, realizing that the man had been shot off the horse with a back wound and then executed as he laid, unable to move, on the ground. Taking time to look for any other tracks, he found where the killer had ridden out and stopped. The man had then returned into the trees. Following his trail, Oli found the men's camp. A second man lay in his blankets, shot through the top of the skull.

An additional search of the camp brought him to where the horses had been picketed for the night. The man out on the grass must have made a break for it, using the dun after his partner had been shot. Oli moved over to the now-cold fire pit. The tracks of three men were in the dust. A half-filled coffee pot sat on a flat stone. A familiar cigar butt lay on the ground next to the fire.

Whoever the third man was, he'd had coffee with the two men before he'd killed them. Oli found where the killer's horse had been tied. There should have been another packhorse, but there was no evidence of one.

The tracks left no doubt that these were the three men whose camp he and Bart had found before arriving at Fort Scott. He remembered the boot prints. One man had worn heels, another a deep groove in the heel, and the third wore narrow boots with sharp edges, which indicated that they were new. Oli went back to check the boots of the two dead men. The narrow boots were not among them.

Checking the two men's pockets, he found an old letter on the first body. It identified this man as Topper. The man in the blankets had only a few coins in his pockets. His saddle had H A P carved into it. They could be initials, or the man's name.

The camp had been occupied for more days than the dead men would have been here. So the fellow with narrow boots had been waiting for them. Waiting for them so he could kill them? It looked like a double-cross. Maybe the third man had not wanted to share the payroll.

Digging two shallow graves, Oli buried the men. There were several stones about, so he collected a good number and piled them onto the mounds. It would slow the wild animals a bit before they dug down to feed on the decaying bodies. Covered with sweat, he removed his hat and sat next to the fire pit to rest. Deer flies flew around his head, landing on his hair. He swatted at them without much success.

Returning to the graves with hat in hand, he bowed his head and said some words over the two men. It was a lonely hillside where these two would spend eternity. Other men would follow him to this area and see the rock-covered mounds, knowing they held bodies, but who they were they would not know. Topper's and Hap's families would wonder what had happened to them and would never know. Oli concluded that this was probably a fitting ending for men like them.

He needed to locate the trail of the narrow boot man and follow it. Before doing that, he took ownership of the coffee pot. Building a small fire, he made a strong brew. The recently departed men had left some supplies behind. The jerky, beans, and cornmeal would extend his rations. There were also two cans of peaches and four bottles of rye. These items Oli had found in a pair of saddle bags, laid over a log, away from the fire. In the killer's haste to ride away, he must have overlooked them.

With the meal finished, and an emptied tin of peaches discarded, he switched his saddle back to the bay. Hap's saddle he put onto the dun, along with the extra saddle bags. He located where the third man had left the area leading an extra horse. The trail continued into the hills, heading northwest.

Oli realized that the man he was following was a cold-blooded killer. He took the Good Knife out of the saddle bag and put it back on the nape of his neck. He checked the loads in the Paterson Colt. The man he was tracking was a day ahead. When they met there was little doubt someone would die. The realization caused tightness in his stomach. He had never felt this type of tension before, not even when lost in the wilderness facing wolves and starvation.

The trail wound through the rolling hills. From one rise he could see a river. The man he followed was not in any hurry. At one point, he had stopped and rested after eating. The horse had grazed a good-sized patch of grass before moving on. He wasn't spending time watching his back trail. The killer was not expecting to have anyone follow him.

It was late afternoon when the trail headed into a valley, toward the river. There were scattered trees between Oli and the water. He decided to stop in a thicket of pecan trees next to a stream that emptied into the river. The location gave him a good vantage point of the river basin below. The trees would help to hide the smoke from his fire.

Breaking up some branches from under the trees, he put a fire together. He set a stone next the flames, then filled his coffee pot and put it to warm. While waiting for the water to heat, he stripped the gear from the horses and gave each a proper rubdown. The contented animals were soon picketed on knee-high grass.

Back at the fire, he added grounds to the boiling coffee water. A quick stir with a spoon prevented the brew from bubbling over. The fry pan full of water and beans sat on the edge of the hot coals. He added a few items from Hap's saddle bags to the beans, then got his coffee mug and one of the bottles of rye.

With coffee laced with rye, he sat back and watched the valley below. In the distance, he could hear crows calling to each other. Honey bees were busy collecting nectar from flowers along the stream. Below, out of sight, the sound of the water cascading over a small falls added to the evening serenade.

The river below reminded him of the Turkey

River that flowed past his home. It was where his pregnant wife, Joan, was waiting for him to return. He thought of how long he had already been gone. It had been almost a month, or maybe a bit more. The days had started running together.

"I am a fool to be out here chasing this man," he softly scolded himself as he sat alone. "If you were smart, Oli August, you would head the horse east and just go home."

"Don't you agree?" he called to the horses. They ignored him.

The smell of the boiling beans got his attention. The juice was bubbling over the edge of the pan and sizzled as it hit the hot embers. Taking his spoon, he mixed them and then scooped some up to taste. Blowing to cool the hot concoction, he took a sip of the liquid, burning his tongue.

"Damn, it's hot." A moment later the aftertaste hit him and he regretted adding small peppers from the dead man's saddle bags. "Yipes, it stays hot too!"

Carefully, he picked the peppers from the pan of beans before starting to eat. By the time supper was done, his forehead was dripping with sweat. At one point he had thought about throwing them out and starting a new batch, but wasting food, especially in the wilds, went against the grain.

Between the peppers and the rye in his coffee, his mouth was on fire. He took a long drink from the stream. It gave little relief.

Sitting against a log, away from the glowing red coals of the fire, Oli gazed into the dark. He was hoping to see a fire below. He poured another measure of rye into his mug and sipped on it while observing the valley and thinking about home. The liquor was relaxing his tired muscles and making his brain a bit fuzzy. He closed his eyes and thought of his children. Karl was a good boy and liked to help his mother. Jenny's help could often make the job harder, but Joan would patiently let the girl participate. Oli wished that he had the type of tolerance she had. His thinking made him unaware of the mosquitoes that were feeding on his exposed skin. Curling up on his side, Oli drifted off to sleep.

CHAPTER TEN

Oli awoke shortly after sunrise. He had a bit of a headache, and the loneliness of being gone from home lay heavily on him. It was time to head for Elkader. Continuing to follow this killer made little sense. There was not much he could do for Martin, anyway. There was plenty that needed to be done back home. The hay had to be made, gardens tended to, and maybe he would finally build the porch on the house. With the decision made, he felt the stress of the past days disappear.

Adding some twigs to the hot ashes, he coaxed the fire back to life. Feeding the flames a bit more wood, he then went to water the horses and move them to new grass. Rinsing the coffee pot, he filled it with water and set it onto the stone. He decided to leave the dun at the first town he came to and then send a telegram to Fort Leavenworth, leaving word for Ernie of the horse's location.

He fried some bacon and mixed up some

sourdough. Putting the dough into the snapping grease, he sat back to wait until the first side was browned. He was humming a Finnish tune his father had liked to sing. It had been a long time since he had last done that. Oli glanced down into the valley and froze for a moment. There was a column of smoke rising from the direction of the river. He guessed it to be about two miles away. Had the air not been still, he would have never seen it.

Oli knew that it should be investigated before heading for home. If it turned out to be some unknown traveler, he would ask if they had seen anyone. With luck they would not have, and he would then continue east.

He took his time with breakfast and stowing his gear. The burning desire to catch up with the man who had killed Topper and Hap was gone. The only thing Oli wanted was to be surrounded by his family. He put the rye bottle into the saddlebags. It was over a third gone.

Grunting, Oli said, "This explains the sore head."

It was mid-morning before he was in the saddle and heading for the river. A breeze had sprung up, dissipating any sign of the smoke. Oli could see a dark line that cut along the hillside above the basin. He guided the horses towards what he figured was a trail.

It was a path that had been made by wildlife heading for water. Oli felt a chill go through him as he also saw the tracks of two horses. Whomever had killed the men he had buried had used this trail. The river could be clearly seen below. If he did come across a camp, then he would have the advantage of the high ground.

Taking his time on the winding trail, it was an hour and a half later before Oli caught the scent of wood smoke. There was a mix of cottonwood and willows just up the valley. It would make a well, secluded camp. He dismounted and tied the horses to a sapling. Checking the load in the Hawken, he then cradled it in his left arm. That would leave the right for drawing the revolver.

The tightness in his stomach that Oli had felt the past couple days returned. Odds were that the occupant of the camp below was the killer. He took his time stalking the camp. When a troop tent came into view, he crouched down behind some low bushes. A man was sitting near the fire, drinking coffee. His back was to Oli. In plain view was a rifle leaning against a boulder, within easy reach. The butt of a revolver showed from his waist band. The killer was well-armed.

Scanning the area around the camp revealed no other occupants. Oli was within an easy shot with the Hawken rifle. He was almost positive that this was the man he was following. The trail had led him to this spot. He hesitated to shoot. It was not in Oli to back shoot a man, not even the killer below.

In some trees, out of view, he could hear horses. One of them would be from the men that this man had killed. The man below was wearing an army jacket and trousers. He must have deserted after stealing the payroll. Taking a deep breath, Oli continued moving down the hill. The Hawken was equipped with dual triggers. The first set the action, the second was a hair trigger and a light touch would fire the rifle. He was stalking with the action set. If the man moved toward the rifle he would touch off a shot at the thickest part of his body.

When he was a dozen paces away, Oli stopped. It was time to let the man know he was caught. It was too late to backtrack and leave. He stomach was fluttering, almost to the point of making him nauseous.

"I've got a rifle with a hair trigger pointed at you. No sudden moves or you will be dead," he said in the most commanding voice he could muster.

The man near the fire lurched forward and then froze as Oli's words sunk in. It took all the control he had to stop from touching off the Hawken and putting a bullet into the man's back. It would have put an end to the danger, but wouldn't help prove Martin's innocence.

"Turn slowly and keep your hands in sight," he instructed his captive.

Slowly, the man turned and faced him. It was Martin!

Shocked, Oli moved the Hawken away from his brother-in-law. He then looked at his boots. They were wide and worn. Relief flooded over him. He realized how close he'd come to shooting first before bracing the man. Also, he had found Joan's brother alive and well. Most of all, the boots were not narrow.

"Oli! Where did you come from? I mean, how . . . how did you find me?" Martin was flabbergasted. He hesitated only a moment before rushing to Oli and hugging him.

Not being comfortable with such a show of emotion, Oli gently pushed Martin to arm's length and desperately searched for a suitable response to the greeting. He mind was full of questions and very confused over where to start.

"Martin, I was following a man and . . . uh, how are you? I was worried about you." He stepped back to gain more distance. He needed some answers from the man in front of him, but first he needed a minute to collect his thoughts. "Let me get my horses. I'll be right back."

Hurrying back to the horses, he took the set off the rifle. Leading the animals back to the camp, he found Martin still standing where he had left him.

"Give me your cup, Oli. I just made some coffee." He reached out his hand for a cup. His expression was one of awkwardness.

Handing him the cup, Oli led the horses to the back of the camp with the other animals. Tying them to a line strung between two trees, he then loosened the cinch straps on both saddles. He took his saddlebags with the spare cylinder back to the fire. Somewhere was the killer. The trail led to this camp. He needed to stay alert.

Martin sat on a log next to the fire and waved Oli over to sit with him. Accepting the steaming cup, he sat next to his brother-in-law. Just as he took a sip, the flap of the tent opened. Startled, he grabbed for his Paterson Colt, spilling hot coffee on himself as a result.

Jumping up, he dropped the coffee and managed to get the revolver out. The shapely figure of Angela appeared. For the second time, he had the drop on someone who did not appear to be a danger to him.

"Oh, Mr. August," she said, putting her hand

to her mouth. "This was unexpected. Please, don't point the gun at me."

"I am sorry, Miss Angela. Your appearance caught me by surprise."

"Do you always greet people that surprise you with a drawn weapon?" she asked sarcastically.

"I do not . . . I." Turning to Martin, he continued, "Have you seen anyone come through here? I have been following a man."

Not wanting to be ignored, Angela answered the question. "My brother came here yesterday. He had to leave, but will be back later this evening."

Martin retrieved his mug and refilled it. "Here you go. I hope you didn't burn yourself too badly." Sitting back down, he continued. "Angela's brother is traveling with us. As you know, it was necessary to escape to prevent being hung. We are heading west to California. Her brother has connections with the Mexican Army and can arrange passage through their territory."

"A man was killed during the escape, Martin," Oli replied, he brow furled. "How did you let this happen? They think I helped you and came after me at Fort Scott."

"The choice I had was to let the man die or get caught and face hanging," Martin said, trying to explain.

"I was looking for the gold and the men that took it," Oli said. "You should have trusted me to prove you innocent."

"I could not wait. When the date is set for the hanging, prisoners are moved to a more secure cell,"

Martin replied, defending his actions. "This would have happened within a day or two. A chance to escape would have been impossible."

"You think your brother-in-law's freedom wasn't worth the cost of a prison guard's life?" Angela asked Oli.

"What freedom?" he demanded. "He now has to give up everything he had in life. Family, friends, not to mention his career." Turning to Martin, Oli added, "You're hiding out here, having to running away to California. How do I explain this to Joan?"

"He is foolish. Don't listen to him, Martin." Turning, she went back into the tent.

Oli glared after her. She was no longer the proper lady he had met at Fort Leavenworth. His mind was racing. Her brother had to be the man who had killed Topper and Hap. Oli was unsure of what he should reveal, even to the man next to him.

He decided to try and get Martin away from these people. "I want you to come with me and we will find the payroll. Then I will bring it back to Fort Leavenworth and at least clear you for the original crime."

"I know where it is, Oli. We have it here in camp."

Oli stared at his brother-in-law, shocked for the second time. How could the gold and silver be here in their camp? For a moment he hoped Angela's brother had taken it from the men he had killed and brought it here. Maybe the two killings were justified.

"You have the money here? And you do plan to return it to the fort?" he said, more as a question than a statement.

"I know that would be the right thing to do, but Oli, you must understand, I will need . . . we, Angela and I, will need the money to live on."

"It is not yours to keep," Oli said, fighting the urge to shout at Martin.

"I was not alone in taking the payroll. There are others to consider."

Dumbfounded, he looked at Joan's brother and saw a stranger. *Did he just say he was in on the robbery?*

"Tell me you misspoke, Martin. You just said that you were part of the robbery!" The heat of anger was soaring through his veins. He realized that he was losing the battle of keeping his voice under control.

"Oli, you don't understand. It is army money. Nobody is hurt by taking it."

"Nobody is hurt! For starters, there was a sergeant that was killed during the act. You have a sister that will never understand how you could do this." Oli was trembling with frustration at what he was hearing.

"I didn't kill anyone. Angela's brother only meant to knock the man out."

"Did you forget about the guard during the escape?" This conversation was going nowhere. Oli was feeling drained.

"The man was going to shoot me. Angela saved my life. She loves me, Oli. I owe her. I know you don't understand, but I owe her that money."

"Do you hear yourself, Martin? You are saying that killing for ill-gotten gains can be defensible?"

Martin continued to try and explain something about doing it for love, about being sorry for the men who had died, but Oli's mind was in a different place altogether. He realized that he was now in the camp of the enemy, and Joan's brother was one of them.

"Martin, come with me to the river and help me get water," Angela said sternly. The men had not noticed her come out of the tent. The look she gave Oli sent chills through him. She was a dangerous woman.

He watched the two of them walk toward the river. She was stepping quickly and Martin was trying to catch up to her. Soon they were out of sight, over the bank. Sitting alone next to the fire, he realized that his coffee had become cold. It did not matter, it was doubtful that he would even have been able to taste the brew.

Oli could hear them talking next to the river but could not make out any of the words. If he was smart, he should get on his horse and ride as fast and far as possible from these people. For a reason that was not clear, he still hoped to save Martin. Maybe it was for Joan, he just was not sure.

All of a sudden, Martin raised his voice and this he heard. "He is my sister's husband." Angela then said something sharply that he could not understand before the level of the conversation dropped.

A voice inside was screaming for him to run, but he sat as though paralyzed, waiting for them to return. Then there was the sound of a horse coming. Removing the loop from his revolver, he stood waiting for the rider to appear. A well-dressed man on a black stallion rode into camp. He had highly polished, narrow boots.

Seeing the blond man standing near the fire, he pulled up and swung down from the horse. After a moment's hesitation, his face broke into a smile and he extended his hand. "Hello, I am Phillip, Angela's brother."

Taking the offered hand, Oli said, "My name is Oli August. Martin is my wife's brother."

Phillip held his hand just a bit too long, as though trying to decide something. He wore his revolver on the left hip. While he held a man's right hand, he could pull the gun. Oli was unsure that he would do so, but after the past things he had learned, he believed anything was possible.

Stepping back, Phillip turned. "Let me take care of my horse and then we can have some coffee." Still smiling, he headed for the horses leading the stallion, leaving behind clear prints of the tracks that had been seen in the camp of death.

The two came back from the river, with Martin carrying a bucket of water. Phillip returned from taking care of his horse and waved at Angela before continuing back to the fire to join Oli. After setting the water down, his brother-in-law added wood to the fire, building it up in preparation for the evening meal.

"What brings you way out here, Oli?" Phillip asked. He stared, waiting for an answer. Maybe he even anticipated the answer.

"I came in search of the payroll. After learning of the escape at Fort Scott, I changed the search to Martin here." His brother-in-law's expression did not give anything away from hearing the explanation.

"Well, you're a lucky man. You have found both right here," Angela's brother said, continuing to smile broadly.

Oli fought to keep his expression neutral. "Yes, Martin has told me you have the payroll."

Brushing a bit of ash from the stoked fire off his pants, Phillip said, "Well, we don't have it all. I had to pay off a couple of partners earlier this week." His mouth was still smiling, but his eyes were as cold as ice and watched Oli for any reaction to the statement.

Angela began to prepare the meal and broke the tension of the moment. Phillip excused himself and said he needed to go and shake the dust of his ride off.

He and Martin were left alone again. Oli wanted to make him aware of the two dead partners he had found. As far as Martin was concerned, the men had been paid and were now off to spend the ill-gotten earnings. He knew that sometime in the future he would find a way to tell him about the two dead men, but now was not the time.

He decided on another tack. "Joan and I have some money put aside. Let us give it to you and Angela to help get your start. I will then bring the remaining payroll back to Fort Leavenworth."

Martin acted like a kid who had just come back from a trip to the woodshed. He was withdrawn and lacked the emotion he'd had before getting the water.

"I couldn't do that to you and Joan. I cannot change what has happened, nor what I have gotten myself into. I believe that once in California, it will all work out."

Oli gave up for the moment and sat staring at the fire as it danced around the wood and embers. If necessary, he would kidnap his brother-in-law in the next few days. Hogtie him and take him away from all this. He hated to think about it, but Martin would be better off at the end of a rope than in the company of these people.

CHAPTER ELEVEN

It turned out that Angela could put out an excellent meal over a campfire. She made a venison stew with potatoes and wild greens. There were golden brown biscuits made in a Dutch oven. It was all complimented with tea and honey.

There was little conversation the rest of the evening. Oli looked around the area, planning his route out when he took Martin away. He watered his horses and picketed them on some grass. When coming back, he passed the washstand. He noticed himself in a mirror that was hanging from a low branch of a tree. His moustache hung over his upper lip. He sorely needed a shave and haircut.

Angela went into the tent right after dark and turned in. Phillip and Martin talked quietly near the horses for almost a half-hour. Meanwhile, Oli sat away from the fire, drinking one last cup of tea. It was good tea, but he missed having coffee.

He made up his bed under a willow tree in the

shadows. Several branches were cut and spread to cushion the area. The ground cloth and blanket were laid over them. He had found a wooden box of cigars in Hap's saddlebags. He took one out and went to the fire and lit it using a burning brand. Moving back under the willow, he enjoyed the pungent smoke. He had been tempted to have some rye, but decided a clear mind was more important than the mellow feeling of the liquor.

He watched as Phillip came back to the fire, picked up the pot of tea and shook it. Finding it empty, he set it down and picked up his bedroll. He made his bed up across the fire from Oli. A few minutes later, Martin came back. He picked up his bedroll and spread it in the same area as Phillip.

Finishing the cigar, Oli walked to the fire and tossed it in. He decided that tomorrow night he would make sure that Martin slept near him and, sometime during the night would make the move to take him away.

Before lying down, he removed the Good Knife and put it under his saddle. He unbuckled his money belt and put it under his blanket. He liked the feel of the gold Spanish coins he carried. He always kept enough for emergencies. It took some time to fall asleep. He realized that he was the outsider of the group. After planning and then re-thinking the grab, he finally drifted off. His dreams brought him home to Turkey River. His son Karl was dragging boards to the front of the house and trying to build a porch. Oli wanted to go and help him, but his legs didn't seem to work.

Sleeping restlessly, he woke once and could

hear the soft snoring of one of the men on the other side of the fire. He could see the red coals of the fire. Rolling over, he soon fell into a deep sleep. Something bumped his leg. Half awake, he thought he was home for a moment and little Jenny was trying to climb into their bed.

"Wake up, Mr. August," Phillip hissed.

Opening his eyes, he saw Angela's brother standing over him with a rifle pointed at his chest. It was just beginning to get light, making the gleeful smile plain to see.

"What are you doing?" he asked.

"You and me are going for a ride. Your brother-in-law will be staying here with Angela."

Sitting up slowly, he saw Martin leading his horse and the black toward him. Phillip stepped back and took the bay's reins. He tossed them to Oli. "Here's your horse. Put the saddle on. Leave the saddle bags and your bedroll."

"Where is my other horse, the dun?"

The question was ignored and Phillip motioned him to move.

As he was getting up, he exposed the money belt so it could be seen. "By the way, toss that belt over here," Phillip ordered.

He picked it up and tossed it in a single motion. Phillip's attention went to the leather belt as he caught it. Oli took the Good Knife out from under the saddle and tucked it behind his waistband, inside his shirt.

While Phillip hefted the belt, liking the weight of it, Oli began to saddle the bay. Positioning the blanket and saddle on the horse, he tried to turn the animal between them. Stepping around the bay, Phillip snorted, "Let's both stay on the same side of the horse."

His wife's brother stood near the tent with Angela. He couldn't believe Martin was letting this man take him out onto the plain at gunpoint. "Don't let him do this. He will kill me."

"You won't be hurt, Oli," Martin assured him. "He will take you to be held by some Mexicans that are friends. In a week, you will be released near the fort."

Looking at his brother-in-law in disbelief, he said, "Is that what they told you? This man killed the men he was bringing the money to. I found and buried their bodies and then tracked him to your camp."

"Don't believe him," Angela told Martin. "I warned you that he would make things up. I know that Phillip took their share of the payroll to them. In fact, he insisted on giving them a little extra."

"Is it necessary to have him taken to the Mexicans? If I told him to go back home, I am sure he would," Martin pleaded.

"Martin, you know we can't take a chance. You don't want him following us and ruining our plans. We are so close to being able to live together in comfort and safety in California."

"Martin!" Oli shouted. "You and I must leave this place now!"

His demand fell on deaf ears. He watched as Angela took Martin's hand and led him toward the river.

"That will be enough, Mr. August. Now get on the horse and lead the way. We are going south about two days. As Martin said, then I will turn you over to some friendly Mexicans. I can assure you they will treat you well."

Looking at Phillip with little confidence that he was being honest, he asked, "Is this the same type of assurances you gave your partners before you killed them?"

"You see what you want, Mr. August. It is true the men are dead, but I only killed one. Topper killed Hap so he could have both shares. I killed him to avenge Hap."

Oli knew better, but realized there was no sense in debating what he clearly saw in the sign left at the camp. Turning the bay, he rode slowly away from the camp. He had been told they would be riding two days south. He would be safe from the man behind him only until they were out of hearing range of a rifle. Anytime after that, he could expect to be back shot.

The sky was clear and the sun hot by mid-morning. His captor did not push him to ride faster. Phillip wanted to stop and rest often. He would have Oli dismount and tie his horse and then move away and sit on the ground. Phillip would then swing down from the black and make himself comfortable, staying at least two horse-lengths away. He would drink water and eat something, never offering any to his prisoner.

This routine continued throughout the day. Once, they stopped at a creek to water the horses. He was allowed to take a drink. Looking at his captor, he asked, "Are you going to offer me something to eat? Or would feeding me be a waste of food?"

"You are too untrusting, Mr. August. The Mexicans will have plenty for you to eat. I, on the other hand, have to conserve my supplies for the ride west. This short duration of discomfort will be soon forgotten."

Oli continued to watch for any chance of escape. The fact that his hands had not been tied gave him some hope that what he was being told might be the truth. He had the Good Knife and could take a chance and throw it at Phillip. The odds of a paralyzing kill were slim. He was never without the rifle and would be able to shoot at least once. It was a risk that he was not ready to take.

"Put that rifle down and step away from it and that will change the odds," he mumbled.

Looking up, Phillip smiled. "You talk. Are you planning on doing something stupid? I should hate to have to kill you. I wouldn't want to carry that news back to your brother-in-law."

It was just before sunset when he was ordered off the bay and told to strip the saddle. The spot was a poor choice for a camp. It was in the wide open plains and the wind would tear at them all night. There was no fuel to build a fire. The heat of the day would soon depart, with the chill of the night settling in.

"Picket your horse over there." Phillip was pointing at a spot 30 feet away.

Taking the time to rub the horse down with handfuls of grass, Oli racked his brain for a way out of this situation. No plan came and he finally returned to his saddle lying on the ground. Phillip remained standing near the black.

"Now, take off your boots and toss them to me. I suggest you get a good night's sleep and then start heading east. You are three days from the Military

Road. Then it is your choice which fort you want to go to."

"It is going to be cold tonight. You didn't let me take my bedroll," Oli reminded him.

"You have your saddle for a pillow and your saddle blanket for a cover. It should make you quite comfortable," Phillip laughed.

Picking up Oli's boots, he swung back up onto the black. "I will be leaving you now. Do not follow me. If I ever see you again, I will kill your brother-in-law. That's after killing you first."

"You had best kill me now. I will never abandon Martin," Oli threatened.

"It would be my pleasure ending your life. But for some reason that I do not understand, my sister loves your Martin and he wants you set free to go home to his sister," he sneered.

Rage surging through his body, Oli fought for control. "Watch your back trail. Soon we will meet again."

"Well, little man, don't look for a fight with me. That is unless, you, are tired of this world." With a laugh that sounded more like a bark, he turned the black. Oli watched him ride past the bay and pull loose the picket rope.

"Walk east, Mr. August," he called, and then rode swiftly away, toward the setting sun, with both horses.

* * *

Phillip was not yet out of sight when Oli made a mental list of his assets. He had the Good Knife and a flint. His clothes were in good repair. The horse blanket would serve as a cover at night and a poncho during the day, if needed. The saddle would provide for his immediate footwear needs.

He muttered as he swung the saddle onto his shoulder and started walking in the direction the man had ridden. "My good man, you may think that taking my boots and horse will stop me from following you. You don't know the little man you left behind."

He walked about an hour in his stocking feet until he felt confident of the direction in which Phillip was heading. He passed an area of switchgrass. It was over four feet-tall and would offer some protection from the wind. He was tired and thirsty. It was near the summer solstice and the days were long. It would be another hour before dark.

Using the saddle, he knocked the grass down, clearing an area for his camp. Setting the saddle upside down in front of him, he began slitting the stitching from the sheepskin lining. This was more than enough to make serviceable moccasins. He cut several strips of leather to be used as ties.

It was fully dark when he completed his footwear. Oli had collected dead switchgrass from the previous year and wound them into tight knots. He had a small fire going using the grass. The light it provided allowed the additional time needed to finish the tasks for tomorrow's travel.

That night he used what was left of the saddle for a pillow. It would now be left behind. He adjusted the horse blanket over his shoulder. Exhausted, Oli was soon asleep.

There was barely enough light to see when he awoke. His throat and mouth felt dry and swallowing was difficult. A constant ache in his stomach reminded him that his last meal had been far too long ago. With his new moccasins on his feet and a bundle of useful items from the saddle, he stepped out briskly, following the trail of the two horses.

Oli placed a flat, smooth pebble into his mouth to try and encourage the saliva to moisten his parched throat. The sun was high and hot when he spotted a distant, dark line on the grassy plain that promised to be a stream or river. He left Phillip's trail and headed directly east toward possible water. It took another hour before Oli reached the trees and was rewarded with a babbling brook. Those first sips would be long remembered. He rested for an hour, taking small drinks until he was finally satisfied.

Phillip's route would cross the brook further to the west. With luck, he would have spent the night near the water. As Oli walked west along the brook he found some edible plants and berries. It was late afternoon when he came across a recent campfire. A quick glance at the debris left behind confirmed that it was his quarry. He was pleased to find an empty peach can. Rinsing the ants from it, he smiled. "This will make an excellent cook pot."

Looking around, Oli decided to spend the night and rest up. It was a good location that offered sources of food. He had found some cattails and dug the roots. These he would bake and eat for dinner. In short order, he had a dozen crayfish boiling in the tin can. He had found them in the rocks along the bank.

Next, he selected several thin willow branches. He fashioned two fish traps like the ones an Indian maiden had taught him to make when he'd been lost in the wilderness some years back. These he set into a deep, slowly moving pool. With luck, breakfast would be broiled fish.

While watching the sun slide down behind the horizon in a large, orange, fiery ball, he worked on building a bow. Selecting several straight boughs, he fashioned some arrows, heat treating the sharpened tips over the glowing coals of his fire. They would be good for bagging small game or birds. Anything bigger would just be sent running with a painful wound.

The next morning the sky was clear, promising a bright, sunny day. The traps had caught three plump suckers. The fish would be quite boney, but a patient eater could enjoy a tasty meal.

He ate two of the fish, and packed one for a midday meal. He would be heading away from the brook. A section of the sheepskin liner had been made into a suitable water bag.

Before leaving, he took his tally book from his shirt and listed his assets. He had food for a day, fish traps, a bow with arrows, a water bag, leather ties, footwear, a container to cook in, a knife, flint, a blanket, and clothing in good repair. He tilted his hat back, adding that to the assets.

He felt that he was equipped for the task ahead. With a little luck, Oli could choose the place of confrontation, therefore improving his chances of a successful outcome. He had accepted the fact that Phillip had to be killed from ambush. Once Phillip was taken care of, he would force Martin to come with him and return to Fort Leavenworth, with or without the stolen payroll.

CHAPTER TWELVE

Oli had been following the tracks of the two horses for two days since leaving the brook. From his belt hung a freshly killed rabbit. It would make a satisfying evening meal. The trail being left meandered, giving the impression of a man who wasn't in any hurry. The direction was generally west. The grass was getting thinner and water less plentiful. The water bag had given up its final drink last night.

Thunderheads were building in the northwest, giving the promise of rain. The days had been hot and a good downpour would be welcome. That is, except for the tracks, which would become more difficult to follow and quite possibly be washed away completely.

Early in the afternoon he came upon water. It was a spring-fed pond surrounded by live oak trees. Abandoning all caution, he tossed down his meager pack and hat. Kneeling, he scooped handfuls of the cool liquid. Suddenly, the water erupted in front of him, followed by the sound of a rifle shot. He threw himself away from the pond and dove behind a spreading oak.

Another shot knocked bark from the trunk, showering Oli with splinters. He curled up on the ground, trying to make himself as small as possible, still unsure of the direction the shooter was firing from. The next several rounds were fired methodically, striking away from his hiding place. Looking around the trunk through some small brambles, he could see a ridge beyond the pond. He was pretty sure that it was the shooter's location.

Again, a bullet struck the tree trunk, forcing Oli to pull back. Several more shots were fired, again away from his location. Realizing that he needed to act, he looked for a way out, keeping the tree between him and the ridge. A rotting windfall laid a few steps behind him. From there it looked like he could move away from the pond and start working his way to safety.

Tensing his muscles, he sprung up into a crouching run. He leaped over the dead tree and slid safely behind it just as a bullet smacked against the decaying wood. Quickly, he moved along the tree toward the upturned root structure. Another searching shot shattered dead limbs. A series of dips and clumps of brush led away from the downed tree.

Oli hid in a wash for an hour, hardly daring to breathe, listening for any sounds of someone moving toward him. Slowly the pounding of his heart subsided. His mind raced. The shooter had to be Phillip. What game was he playing? Believing that Phillip was farther ahead of him, Oli had been obviously careless approaching the water. Why hadn't the man just finished him while he was in the wide-open?

After another half-hour, his leg cramping from crouching in the wash, Oli crawled out. He had to find out if the shooter had left. Cautiously working his way away from the pond and wide of the ridge, Oli could feel the sweat running down his body. The tension was acute, as he expected a shot in his direction at any time. The ridge was just over 400 feet from his original location at the pond.

Oli found a cut that ran toward the ridge and painstakingly worked his way along its bottom, fearful every time he had to look over the edge. It seemed like an eternity, and he had covered less than half the distance. He came to an open area that would leave him exposed for several seconds, plenty enough time for the shooter to take aim and fire.

The thirst had returned. The few handfuls of water had given little lasting relief. Going back to the pond was not an option. Leaving without his hat and pack was also not a choice, so at some time he would have to return to where he had left them. It was still several hours until dark. There had been no more shots after he had left the dead tree. It was possible that the shooter had gone. Then again, he could be patiently waiting for his target to appear.

Laying in the shallow cut, Oli searched the ridge for any sign. Something caught his eye. It was just a glimpse of movement. It was to the left, along the ridge. Could it have been his imagination? Maybe the stress of the situation was getting to him. There it was again . . . something.

Unexpectedly, he saw a small, dark object fly into the air. It was followed by a silver fox. The young fox had a field mouse and was playing with it as it moved along the ridge. He quickly realized that whoever had been on that ridge had left. The fox had a clear view behind the rise and saw no danger.

Steeling his nerves, Oli moved across the opening in a low lope. Gaining the crown of the ridge, he laid down and looked for signs of the shooter. The fox continued over the ridge, heading for the pond and a drink of water.

Moving along the ridge, he found the abandoned location of the shooter. Gun stock imprints in the dust revealed that two rifles had been used. There had also been a revolver for the multiple shots. Narrow foot prints leading away from the ridge confirmed the shooter as Phillip.

Oli knew that the shots had been a warning. He could have easily killed him with the first bullet. Slowly, the understanding came to him that the trail had not been aimless. Angela's brother had been searching for a spot to set up and wait to see if he was followed.

His parched throat reminded him that water was a short distance away. Taking another moment, he found where the horses had been tied. Their droppings confirmed that the wait had been several hours.

Remaining cautious, Oli went back over the hill. He returned to the pond and drank. Glancing at his pack, his jaw dropped. Both the hat and pack were riddled with bullet holes. Was that the objective of the shooter, to keep him down while destroying the gear?

The rumble of thunder went unnoticed as Oli went through his pack. The can had a tear in the bottom along with other holes. It was ruined. The bow was fractured, and one fish trap broken. The water bag was of the most concern. Two bullets had gone through it and at best it would only hold one cup of water after being repaired.

He was looking over his hat when the first drops of rain hit him. Clamping it down over his head he thought, *With all the holes, any rain that runs in will run back out.*

Chain lightning gave a spectacular show as the fast-moving storm swept across the plains. Oli knew that there was danger sitting under a tree during a thunder storm, so he moved away from the pond and found a depression left by the roots of the fallen tree. Sitting tight against the root ball offered some protection from the wind-blown rain.

The rain came in fast, and was of short duration. The sun came out as the clouds passed, making everything steamy. He could hear the rush of water in the distance. Some normally dry riverbed had come back to life after the storm. Oli was exhausted and decided to make camp near the fallen tree.

It was getting dark by the time that the rabbit caught earlier was roasting over the fire. Oli had already used an oak branch to fix the bow. The remaining fish trap had been set into the pond. One of the moccasins that had a seam ripped open when he'd been forced to dive for cover was repaired. The sheep skin was wearing thin and would not give him many more days of service.

As he chewed the nicely browned rabbit, he evaluated his assets. The rabbit skin drying on an oak ring was added. The cooking container was taken away, along with one trap. His blanket was in a little rougher shape, but still serviceable. His final conclusion was that he was still equipped for the task ahead.

Oli knew that he should forget Martin and head east. He believed Joan would understand him taking that action. But two thoughts went through his mind. He would have to live with the pain his wife would experience at the disgrace of her brother, and those who caused it would go free. Oli realized that there was no turning back.

Today's setback had been a lesson. He realized that immediate needs had trumped caution. He had focused on the water, forgetting about what had surrounded the pond. There could have been hostile Indians or wild animals nearby. In his haste, no time had been taken to look. Oli had been lucky that it was Phillip just wanting to discourage him from continuing.

The chilling realization was that he was being toyed with, like a fox with a mouse. It was quite possible Phillip wanted him to follow and would then kill him as he got close to his sister. He could then say he did everything possible to deter Oli, but unable to do so, was forced to kill him.

With the stars large in the night sky, he covered himself with the slightly damp, bullet-riddled blanket. The peeper frogs were loud around the pond. A lone bull frog called into the night. Out on the plains coyotes howled as they searched for prey.

He gradually had come to realize that unlike the last time he'd been in the wilderness, these sounds didn't frighten. Rather, they told him that he was safe from anyone stalking him. Furthermore, he could make fire and catch game with hand-made traps or weapons, so starving could be avoided.

He slept lightly and woke several times to the sounds of animals coming to the pond for a drink. Once, he came wide awake when hearing splashing and growling when a wolf or coyote took down a thirsty animal across the pond. A glance at the stars told him that it would be another couple of hours before daylight. At first light, he was ready to get up.

The trap had a nice-sized catfish. It made a satisfying breakfast. He missed having morning coffee. Had the can been available, he could have roasted some acorns and brewed a hot drink. It would not have been as good as coffee, but better than nothing. He tied his pack together and slung it over his shoulder. The filled water bag hung at his waist. Picking up the new and improved bow, he took a moment to flex it. The oak made a stronger weapon. With a little better arrow, he was confident that it would bring down a small deer or antelope.

Taking a final long drink, he looked to the west and the rolling plain. Phillip had been leading him in a westerly direction. If Angela was taking Martin to California, they would be going by way of Santa Fe. When he had gone west some years back, those he'd gone with had followed the route along the Platte River, with Oregon being their destination.

The rain would have washed some of the tracks out and make following Phillip difficult. If the trail was easily found, then he could be sure that a trap lay ahead. With his mind made up, he headed directly west. He hoped to cross the Santa Fe Trail within two days. It was doubtful that Martin and Angela were very far away. Phillip knew this, thus his lack of urgency to get back to them.

By early the second day, Oli came across a trail cutting across the plains that was reminiscent of the Oregon Trail. He was sure that it was the Santa Fe Trail. There were not any tracks from the past few days, so if they were following it, he should now be ahead of them. A cluster of boulders with a spring lay within eyesight of the trail. He set up camp there to wait.

He had managed to kill a young deer the day before and had the remaining meat wrapped in the hide. With his meager camp set up, he began to jerk the venison. His blanket was filled with buffalo chips and pieces of wood he had found along the way.

As the smoke drifted through the meat, preserving it, he looked over his footwear. A hole, as big as the end of his thumb, had worn in the bottom of one of the moccasins. He would use the deer hide to repair it.

He had scraped the hide and rubbed it with the animal's brains and bone marrow the night before. Now he used urine to remove the oils. By evening the stretched hide was leaned over the fire to allow the smoke and heat to speed the drying.

After three days alongside the Santa Fe Trail, he began to second-guess his strategy. It was possible that the others had passed further north. While worrying about missing Martin's group, he kept busy. The sheepskin footwear had been replaced with deerskin moccasins. A new water bag and a small pack for carrying food were made. Each day he had added fresh meat from hunting.

To keep mobile, the gear was kept packed for easy carrying. He spent nights away from the spring. It might be known by Phillip, therefore a destination. He didn't want them to discover his camp and give away his whereabouts. One evening, when returning to re-supply his water he'd found tracks of unshod ponies near the spring. It reminded him that there were other dangers, not just Phillip.

Returning from a hunt with two bagged prairie dogs, he stopped shy of the rise above the spring. After being surprised at the pond, he no longer skylined himself without taking time to make sure there was no danger about.

It had been six days since he had arrived in the area. As his gaze moved from storm clouds developing in the west to the spring, he caught his breath. There was smoke rising from behind the boulders. The back of a covered wagon was partially visible. Someone had made camp at the spring. The presence of a wagon made him unsure if it was Martin.

He settled in to wait and watch. He knew that this was Mexican territory. If he was caught by their army, he would be made a prisoner and taken south. There was enough water in the bag, so getting to the spring tonight was not necessary.

Moving a safe distance from the campers, Oli found a secluded spot to skin and roast the dogs. When the sun was low in the sky he put the fire out. He didn't want a possible wanderer from the spring to spot the flames.

At first light in the morning, Oli was lying on the rise near the spring. He could hear voices below, but they were too far away to understand. The sounds of horses being hitched to the wagon could be heard. A short man with stooped shoulders and a white beard appeared near the wagon. He placed a cook pot and his bed roll into the back. He called to someone out of sight, near their fire.

A slender man stepped out. It was Martin! Oli's heart pounded with excitement. He fought down the urge to call out. He did not fear Angela, and the man, or men, who had the wagon had no fight with him. But, somewhere below, was Phillip. He must be dealt with first.

Martin tossed a bed roll and a bundle that was most likely the tent onto the wagon as he walked back around. A few minutes later, the wagon started to move. Leading the group was Phillip on the black, followed by Martin riding the bay and leading a pack horse. Angela sat on the wagon between the bearded man and another short, husky, red-headed man.

Oli lay on the ridge, watching as the group moved out onto the plains. Phillip was riding out checking both sides, scanning the surrounding area. He had to wait until they were some distance away before going back to the spring for water.

Taking only a moment to glance over their camp, he hurriedly filled the water bag and took a drink of water. He wished that there was more time to drink his fill, but his quarry was moving away. He stopped when he saw empty tin cans that were tossed away from the fire. They had several holes from a knife, rendering them useless for use as a cook pot, no doubt Phillip's work.

After checking to make sure that the horizon was clear, he left the shelter of the boulders near the spring and started after the wagon at a trot. Throughout the morning, he would stop as soon as he saw the top of the wagon canvas and wait for it to disappear before moving on. Just after midday, a tree-lined stream in a valley came into view. The wagon turned toward it.

As he watched, Oli swore and flattened himself on the ground. Phillip and the black were missing. Sometime between the last sighting and now, he had left the group. A prickly feeling went up his back. The man who wanted to kill him was out there someplace. It was possible that he had gone ahead and was waiting for them at the stream. Or, he might be waiting for Oli to expose himself.

Lying in the grass a quarter-mile away from the water, he watched the wagon stop near a group of willows. He observed people below as they watered the animals and started a cook fire. All movement was routine. No one was watching for Phillip to return. Just maybe he was off hunting, or had ridden ahead with plans to meet them in the evening.

Glancing around, he saw what might be a pothole, or a spring with a stand of buttonbush. The group below wouldn't be visible from the bushes, but he wouldn't exposed. It would offer some cover in case the missing Phillip was checking their back trail.

Staying low and using patches of Indian grass for cover, he worked his way to the low bushes. Settling among the buttonbush, he caught the fragrance of the spherical white flowers. Feeling safe for the moment, Oli figured that he'd better eat something. It could be a long time before he had another chance.

Setting his bow and arrows within easy reach, he dug into his food bag. He took out some leftover prairie dog from the night before. The cold, stringy meat took some chewing. He used the Good Knife to slice small pieces.

Sitting cross-legged in the middle of the cluster of bushes, he picked up the water bag to wash down the dog. He felt the tug on the bag a split second before hearing the shot. Water splashed onto his face and ran down on his pants. As a reflex action, he threw the bag and rolled, picking up the bow. Standing just inside the buttonbush perimeter was Phillip. He held Oli's Colt Patterson loosely in his right hand. There was a broad, taunting smile on his face.

"Caught you napping again, little man," he laughed.

Twice now, he had surprised Oli while quenching his thirst. His arrogance was maddening. He stood in the open, plainly in control of the situation.

"Where's your horse?" Oli asked in a conversational tone.

The casual attitude angered Phillip. He knew that he could kill this aggravating man following them with a quick shot from the revolver. "Where my horse is at is the last thing you should be wondering about."

"I was concerned that you might have lost it. I will need the black when I ride out of . . ." Without finishing the sentence, Oli brought the bow up and shot an arrow at Phillip.

The arrow struck the upper right of the man's chest. He had tried to dodge the arrow, jumping to the side, but had been too late. Remarkably, he kept control of the gun. There was no time or place for Oli to dodge to get away.

Phillip pulled the crude arrow from his chest, the wound bleeding freely. It did not immobilize or even seem to hamper the man.

Training the gun on Oli, he said, "Goodbye, Mr. August."

Phillip jerked suddenly and Oli steeled himself for the impact of the shot. It did not come. Instead, the big man slowly turned, exposing a yellow and black feathered arrow in his back. He had been shot by an Indian!

As Phillip sank to his knees, he dropped the Colt Patterson. Oli abandoned his bow and crawled past the stricken man, scooping up the revolver. Keeping low within the flowering bushes, he moved toward the perimeter. Behind him he could hear the plea for help.

"Don't . . . don't leave me. I need help. August! Come back!"

Never in his life had Oli ignored a person in trouble. Near the edge of the buttonbush grove, he crouched and looked out, searching for the brave. He could hear the coughing and choking sounds from Phillip. The arrow must have hit a lung and the dying man was drowning in his own blood.

Shutting out the agonized sounds, he focused on the unseen danger somewhere on the grassy plain. He needed to find Phillip's horse. There must be a dip near the grove where he had hidden the animal. "Where is your damn horse?" Oli muttered.

Oli knew he'd be a fool and would probably

lose his hair wandering around looking for the horse. For all he knew, it might have already been taken by the Indians. Oli knew his only chance was to go back and ask the dying man.

Crawling through the brushes, he worked his way back to Phillip. For a moment, he thought that he was too late. His legs twisted below his body, Phillip lay still, eyes open to the sky. Moving up slowly, Oli searched for danger. All he saw was gently swaying grass from the opening beyond. His bow and packs lay where he had left them.

Coming up to Phillip, he noticed bubbling from the wound. The sucking wound told him that the man had not yet died.

Crouching near, he whispered, "Where is your horse? I can't help you without it."

He knew that he was lying to the man. There was no helping Phillip. He had little time left. Oli's hope sank as he looked at the unresponsive man.

Then the eyes fluttered. The raspy voice was weak. "Leave me. Go help . . . Angela."

"Your horse, I need your horse," he urged.

"Just . . . just south of he . . .re," His voice faded and the unseeing eyes continued to stare at the sky.

Taking just a second to strip the holster with its pouch for reloading the revolver from the dead man, he went to find the horse.

Stopping another instant, he glanced at the man's boots. "Damn, you would have such small feet."

Keeping within the buttonbush, he moved toward the south side. The bush turned into a swamp fed by the spring. The wet area was lined with cattails.

Wading through the water and muck along the edge, he continued until he found a cut made from heavy rains that led toward what he hoped was a dip.

Emerging from the swampy area, he crawled into the shallow washout. Oli used it to conceal his movements as he looked for the black.

A snort alerted him that the animal was nearby. The cut expanded into a broad gully. There the black stood, tied to a low bush. Its head was up, watching the opposite side. Oli searched for danger. Suddenly, a Cherokee appeared from the scrubby grass. The brave moved toward the horse, trying to calm it with soft words.

On his back was a quiver of arrows with yellow and black feathers. It had to be the Indian who'd shot Phillip. The brave must have seen Phillip come and then followed him. After putting an arrow into him, the Indian had come back for the black.

There was a whisper of sound behind Oli, warning him of danger. Throwing himself to the side, he rolled just in time to avoid the tomahawk swung by another Cherokee. The weapon sent sparks as it struck rocks.

The move to avoid the attack pinned the Colt Patterson under his body. As the brave rose to take a second swing to crush his prey's skull, Oli drew the Good Knife from the nape of his neck with his left hand and thrust it into the Cherokee's stomach, ripping upward as it sunk in. The brave wilted as he came forward, collapsing on top of him.

Panic rose in Oli as he realized that there was still another Cherokee, both of his arms were pinned and he was wedged in the cut. Squirming and kicking, he threw the dead man off, freeing the revolver, and turned in time to see a yellow and black feathered arrow, notched and drawn back by the other Indian.

Ducking back, he instinctively fired a shot. An arrow struck the side of the wash, spattering Oli with dirt. He looked over the edge of the wash, aiming the Colt Patterson in the direction of the Cherokee, but he saw nothing but an empty space. The shot had turned the black's attention in his direction. He had no idea where the Indian had gone.

Straining his eyes for danger, he moved toward the horse. Using a rock outcrop for protection, Oli expected the brave to appear at any time. The area did not offer many places to hide. The Cherokee may have gone back onto the grassy plain to work his way around and catch him from an unexpected direction.

All of Oli's senses began to tingle, expecting an arrow any second. His inability to stay put saved his life. Leaping up, he ran toward the black. Grabbing the reins, he ducked under the neck of the horse and swung into the saddle from the far side. Digging his heels into the flanks of the nervous animal, it sprung forward up the side of the dip, reaching the top at a full gallop.

Something flashed by his head as he leaned low over the neck of the running black. He turned the horse toward the wagon. To his left were four mounted Cherokee, intent on cutting him off. The black ran like the wind, smooth, strong, outdistancing the Indian ponies. He shouted at the unsuspecting group, "Indians, take cover, Indians!"

CHAPTER THIRTEEN

The galloping horse charged into the camp, Oli pulling it to a stop. Leaping to the ground, he grabbed the saddlebags from the horse and ran for the cover of some fallen trees where Martin and Angela had set up a defense. The white-bearded man had just finished hitching the team. The sudden appearance of Oli on the black, and the cries of the attacking Cherokee, startled them and the horses lunged ahead, taking the wagon out onto the plain, away from the safety of the wooded area.

The old man grabbed onto the wagon and climbed into the seat, struggling with the reins, trying to stop the horses. A brave rode alongside the wagon and put an arrow into the lower back of the man. He slumped over in the seat as the Cherokee continued to drive the panicked horses and wagon away.

Oli looked up and saw the wagon quickly putting distance between them. He heard a shout up the stream. The stocky, redheaded man was running towards them clutching a fishing pole in his hand. He had wandered too far from the camp to fish. A Cherokee was cutting him off and swinging a tomahawk.

The group watched in shock as the brave swung and the top of the man's red hair seemed to fly up from the top of his head. As the struck man's knees buckled, the sound of Martin's rifle exploded alongside Oli. The shot was true, knocking the brave from his horse.

Martin tossed the empty weapon to Oli. "Load it and make every shot count," he commanded. "Angela, you keep loading rifles and revolvers as we fire." He pointed at a short-barreled shotgun leaning against the windfalls. "If they get into the perimeter, use that. The buckshot will cut a wide swath."

Turning his attention back to the attacking Cherokee, he did a quick assessment. "I figure there are around a dozen Cherokee. Most went after the wagon and team. The rest are staying out of range, making sure we remain pinned down."

Oli was pleased to see that the rifle was his own Hawken .50 caliber. While loading the weapon, he watched Martin's cool actions. His military training and abilities showed well. He glanced at Oli and then went to help Angela set up the loading station. Could three of them fight off so many braves? Maybe Martin's experience would be enough.

Oli began to go through the saddlebags. He found the spare cylinder for the Colt-Patterson. It was fully loaded. He found additional powder and ball for the revolver. He also had some in the pouch on the holster. He watched the plain while loading the empty chambers of his revolver.

An unnerving scream came from up the stream. It had to be the redheaded man. He had not been killed by the blow and was now being set upon by the Cherokee. The three of them looked in the direction of the cries of pain, but could not see anyone. The cold realization was that it could soon be them suffering at the hands of the hostiles.

For the next half-hour they endured the cries of the unfortunate man. They had spotted smoke in that direction. Evidently, fire was being used. Martin continued to set up their defenses, barking orders at Oli and Angela. Depending on him, they were quick to follow his commands. The thick willow trees along the stream and fallen branches protected the rear. They had a clear field of fire on three sides.

Martin and Angela had grabbed enough water, food, and ammo when they saw Oli riding for his life from the attack. It was enough to put up an extended defense. With as much improvement to their fortification as possible, it was decided to eat while they had a chance. Shortly, the Cherokee would focus on them and it might be a long time before their next meal. Angela began to put a small fire together and heat water for coffee. Soon the aroma of the brew, as well as bacon, filled the area. The two men were on watch. Oli smelled the cooking and could not stop his mouth from watering. It had been some time since he had enjoyed anything other than unseasoned wild game and plants.

They ate the bacon with biscuits, washed down with coffee while remaining at their posts. Other than giving necessary orders, Martin had not spoken to him.

While eating, Angela sat next to him and they spoke softly. By the tone, Oli was sure that he was trying to comfort her.

"When do you think they will attack?" he asked Martin, more to start conversation than anything else.

The young lieutenant looked at his brother-in-law. "It is three, maybe four hours before dark. When the sun is low in the western sky, we can expect them to come. It will be from that direction."

Angela got up and went to check on the horses that had been brought into the trees behind them. It was clear that she was giving them room to talk.

"If we get out of here, Martin, I want you to come back with me to Fort Leavenworth. Angela is welcome to come also."

"What has become of Phillip? He won't let her go." Martin did not look at Oli, but kept his eyes on the plain.

"He is dead. One of the Cherokee put an arrow in his back." The modified version was best for now. He heard a stifled cry from the direction of the horses.

"She and I have no future at the fort. We would both be jailed and more than likely scheduled to hang."

He then turned and looked Oli in the eye. "If we get out of this, I will send you back with the money. Angela and I will continue west."

Taking his wife's brother back was still his intention. Debating that with him now would be pointless. Giving back the money was an important step, a good start.

Angela came back to her station. She had been crying. In a controlled voice she said, "The horses are set and ready to ride if necessary."

The three sat in silence, each in their own thoughts as they awaited their fate.

* * *

It was two hours before dark, with the sun low in the western sky, when they started hearing cries from the Cherokee. The cries were signals to coordinate their attack. Two braves came over the rise to the southwest. They cut across the grassy plain, making shrill yells that sent chills up Oli's back.

"Only shoot at them if they get close. They are a distraction. The attack will come from the sun," Martin warned.

As if on cue, the remaining Cherokee came fast and hard out of the west. The sound of their running horses were heard first. Then as they got closer, they broke into a chorus of yells. The two men sighted their rifles on the charging braves. Oli fired and saw a Cherokee jerk and cling to his pony to prevent falling off.

"Take your time, settle on a target, and fire," Martin instructed as he squeezed off a shot. A brave fell from his horse.

There were three rifles. Angela would load the extra rifle while the men fired. While waiting for another rifle, they would shoot the revolvers. They kept a steady field of fire that broke the first attack. At least two Cherokee had been shot off their ponies. A wounded animal lay kicking on the grass.

The second attack came from the front, with the Cherokee splitting to both sides. They were riding low and keeping most of their bodies behind their horses. As they swept past the fortification, a hail of arrows were let go from under the horses necks, with many landing within the defenses. The men fired, unable to line up on any good targets. One horse was knocked down and the rider climbed on with another rider.

Quickly, all their weapons were reloaded and they readied for the next attack. The waiting made time drag. They stared at the empty plain, knowing that danger was hiding out there. Martin knew this strain of waiting was the worst part of battle. He thought of something to help.

"Angela, stoke up the fire and put on more coffee. My guess is the Cherokee have been testing our fire power and will plan a new strategy before coming again."

Nodding, she moved as if in a trance over to the fire and added kindling to the coals. Her face was drawn and her eyes were showing fear.

"Oli, make sure all the powder and bullets are at the loading station. Also, take a little more time choosing your targets. We don't want to empty weapons without a hit. If you can't line up on a Cherokee, aim at their horses. Remember, a hit every shot."

His ears were still ringing from the shots fired. He knew that the advice from Martin was sound. He had wounded one Indian during the first wave and had had clean misses with the second wave.

Watching his brother-in-law take charge made him proud to be fighting alongside him. It was unfortunate that his career in the army was over. He had been misused as a pay officer. He should've been leading patrols against marauding hostiles.

"When this is over, I still want you to come back with me. We can drop Angela off someplace so she can go back to New Orleans," Oli suggested.

"You love my sister. Would you consider leaving her as you are asking me to do so?" Martin asked.

"No, I couldn't."

"You have to understand, Oli. I love Angela as much as you love Joan. Stealing the payroll was a mistake. As I said, you can take the money back to the fort. You must see my position on this."

At this point, Oli knew Martin was not coming back. Deep down, he felt a relief. Bringing his brother-in-law back to Fort Leavenworth could only result in his being hanged.

"I do understand, Martin. I will take back the payroll and do my best to explain what happened when I get back to Joan. While the crimes you have committed will hurt her, your being hung would be many times worse."

"Thank you, Oli," he said, smiling for the first time.

"Your coffee." Angela's voice broke the moment. Oli accepted the cup. Sipping it gave little pleasure. The stress of the attack left him without an appetite for anything. He set it down and returned to looking at the plain.

She brought Martin his cup and they sat, talking in low tones. She was unhappy about something. The lieutenant put his arm around her, pulling her close. Softly, he was assuring her of something.

The minutes dragged by as they watched and waited for the next attack. Their cups lay next to the dying coals of the fire. Each sat at their post.

The grass moved slowly in the late afternoon breeze. Shadows appeared and disappeared. Oli watched for any sign of the returning Cherokee. Despite the breeze, he was sweating. It trickled down under his shirt. His eyes burned as sweat ran down his brow.

Something was wrong in front of him, but he couldn't put his finger on it. His eyes began to blur. Rapid blinking was not helping. He reached for his canteen to rinse his face when one of the shadows rose. With a shrill cry, the Cherokee leaped forward, firing his bow as he ran.

Oli swung his Hawken rifle and fired. Pointing, rather than aiming, at the moving target brought success. The brave collapsed in a heap short of the barrier, his yellow and black feathered arrows spilling from the quiver.

Setting the rifle down for Angela to load, he raised his revolver and began to fire at the closest shadows. A grunt and then the sound of a man moving through the grass confirmed that he'd gotten a hit.

"Martin!" Angela cried.

Oli looked over and saw an arrow in his upper chest, with the point protruding out of his back near the shoulder blade.

Oli began to move toward his brother-in-law. "No, Oli. Stay at your post. I am hit, but can still fire. Angela, keep loading the weapons."

The sun began to slide behind the horizon. No more Cherokee appeared. Martin had told him that if they could hold out until dark, they would be safe until daylight. This would allow them to take turns resting.

Angela heated water to be used after the arrow was removed from Martin. She tossed dirt over the fire to ensure that their movements couldn't be seen by the Cherokee. Oli crawled over to his brother-in-law. In the low light, he could see the pain on his face. His breathing was labored.

"We'll get the arrow out. I can make a poultice that will help prevent infection," he said with less confidence than his voice reflected.

"My legs were cramping . . . I rose for just a moment to get relief. He was . . . just waiting for one of us to show." Finishing the sentence, he stifled a groan. Trying to talk was painful.

Angela came over with the hot water, setting it down beside the lieutenant. She laid out some strips of cloth to be used for a bandage.

"We have to cut the tip off the arrow to pull it out. We should have done this immediately. The flesh will have tightened around the shaft." The last part she said more to Martin than Oli. He had not let her help him until the sun went down.

Quickly, she began taking care of the injury. Instructing Oli to cut the arrow shaft with his razor sharp Good Knife, she then held his shoulders while Oli withdrew the yellow and black feathered arrow. He could feel it tearing at the flesh inside as it broke loose and started to slide out. Martin let out a ragged, long moan and fell silent. He had passed out from the pain.

Once the shaft had been removed, Angela applied pressure to the front, while he placed his palm on the back opening to stop the bleeding. After several minutes, they turned him onto his side so the wounds could be cleaned and bandaged.

Sitting back a bit, Oli listened to the night sounds. They were normal night sounds. All was undisturbed outside their fortification. Inside, the horses shifted occasionally. A coal missed by the dirt would glow as a gust of breeze found it. The night sounds were broken only by the shallow breathing of the wounded man.

Exhausted, Angela moved back to get some sleep. Oli moved over to Martin. The lieutenant had not regained consciousness since passing out. When adjusting the blankets, he felt the wetness of the bandages. The wounds were still bleeding.

Sitting back, he bowed his head and prayed for Martin. He felt helpless to aid his brother-in-law. He prayed for strength to face the days to come and promised to bring him back to the fort where there were doctors.

A slight noise outside the fortification turned his attention to the inky darkness. Could the Cherokee be doing the unexpected and attacking at night? He wished that the moon would light the plain. The bright stars overhead did not offer much illumination.

Hunkering down and clutching his Hawken .50 caliber, Oli searched the dark plain for any sign of movement. He knew one should not shoot at shadows, but he decided that if he saw any hint of motion, he would fire.

He noticed that the crickets had fallen silent. Nervous energy was making his hands clammy. He wiped them on his shirt. He felt the need to move, in case whoever was out there had pinpointed him. Unable to locate the danger, he dared not try and move for fear he would make noise. He fought to keep his breathing even to help quiet his pounding heart. It was loud in his ears and Oli was sure everyone around could hear it.

"Oli, Oli are you there?"

The sound of Martins voice almost made him jump out of his skin. Fighting to compose himself, he forcing his voice to be soft and calm, "I am here, Martin."

With a weak, hoarse voice, the wounded man continued. "I am sorry I put you in this position."

"It's all right, Martin."

He felt the man's hand grab his arm. "No . . . no, it's not. I was selfish and now your life is in danger."

"You are family, Joan's brother. I would not even consider not being here."

"I want you to do me a favor. Before daylight, take the horses and our supplies and make a run for it with Angela." His voice was becoming weaker, almost a hiss.

"I can't do that."

"The Indian, that . . . that shot me. He had figured out our defense." Martin was silent a moment before continuing. "He had seen me as the strength. He needed to kill me so the rest would fall. He had figured on you missing the shot and him getting away."

"Don't try and talk, Martin," Oli urged.

Ignoring the request, he said, "You got him for me, Oli."

Martin began coughing and gasping for breath. After a minute or so, he was able to talk again. "I owe you now. You have to save yourself and Angela. I am a dead man already. Let me stay behind and cover your escape."

Again, he began to cough until exhausted, then he fell silent.

Oli didn't know if he was even conscious anymore. In the darkness, he sat listening to the shallow breathing. As the night dragged on, his eyes became heavy. He should wake Angela and get some sleep himself. In a moment, he would do that. Right now he wanted to stay near Martin.

He didn't know how long he had been asleep, when his eyes opened. He held his breath. Something was wrong. It was still dark, the crickets were singing loudly. He strained his ears to try and hear what was out of place. A wolf howled out on the plain.

Abruptly, he knew. He couldn't hear Martin's breathing! He reached out to make sure the man hadn't moved. He felt the still body beside him. Slowly, he moved his hands over the head and neck, looking for any sign of life. Martin was gone.

All the feelings of the night came out in tears. Stifled sobs wracked his body. Finally, drained of all emotion, he sat thinking of the pain in store for his wife. He sat thinking about all that had happened. He continued to reflect until the first light came up in the east.

Looking over at Martin, he saw a man in peaceful sleep. The peace that comes when life's battle is over.

The rustle of skirts caught his attention. Angela was awake.

"You should have woken me for my watch," she said, glancing at the cold fire.

She then hurried to see how Martin was. As she knelt, a cry of realization came.

"Oh my god. Martin! Dear Martin." She threw herself on his chest, burying her face and weeping.

Oli looked out onto the grassy plain. It would not be long before the Cherokee would return. Would the two of them have the will to fight on? He almost gasped when noticing that the body of the brave who had shot Martin was gone. He remembered the crickets falling silent last night. It had to be when the others were removing the fallen man. Realization that the Cherokee had been so close left him shaken.

They sat in the early hours, each mourning the loss in their own way. Oli prayed for the questionable soul of his brother-in-law, while Angela sat in stony silence, holding the cold hand of her lost love.

The sun was high in the morning sky before Oli moved to make a small fire and get coffee going. He had watched for any sign of the Cherokee. The expected attack had not come with the rising sun. It appeared that the conflict might be over.

Maybe the loss of life had been too high for them to continue. Or, maybe they had gotten enough scalps and goods to declare the attack a success and were now on the way back to sing of their deeds around the council fire.

He drank coffee and chewed jerky as he planned their next move. Angela had refused to eat or drink anything. It was time to bury the dead. He wished that Martin could be taken back to Elkader or even Fort Leavenworth for burial. Doing so was not practical.

Gulping down the last of his coffee, Oli rose and walked to the large windfall that made the main wall of the fortification. He hoped to find a shovel on the wagon. He wanted Martin buried deep, away from the digging varmints of the plains.

"I'll check out the wagon and bring the other bodies back here so we can bury them decent."

If Angela heard him, he couldn't tell. She made no move to acknowledge. Riding his bay and leading the black, he rode slowly toward the wagon. While he was now exposed to danger, it felt good to be out in the open on the back of a horse. It gave him a better vantage point to watch for trouble.

The wagon had been stripped and burned. The team was gone and the gruesome remains of the bearded man lay a short distance away, covered with buzzing flies. He found a shovel that had some charring on the handle. It would still be usable for the task at hand.

Taking one of the blankets he had brought for the purpose, he wrapped the body and slung it over the back of the black. He then found Phillip where he had left him. He had also been stripped and scalped. His eyes and genitals had been removed. Again, bluebottle flies were busy laying eggs in the bloody wounds. Wrapping him in the same manner as the first man, he thought, *I just hope those narrow boots create bunions on the Indian that got them.*

He wouldn't have known the last body was the redheaded man. After scalping him, they had suspended him over a low fire and let him slowly burn to a crisp. The stocky body was now a thin, blackened horror. As he wrapped the man, it bothered Oli that he could smell the aroma of cooked meat. It was a memory that would be a long time going away.

Returning back to their camp with the bodies and shovel, he was surprised to find Angela busy making rolls in the Dutch oven. A fresh pot of coffee was bubbling next to the fire and strips of bacon were sizzling in a cast iron skillet.

Glancing at Martin's body, he saw that he lay uncovered with the bloody bandages drawing insects. Swinging down from the bay, he brushed the flies away and covered the body with a blanket.

"The meal will be ready in a minute. We best have a good feed before getting started."

She spoke as though nothing had happened. Confused, and a little angry, Oli grabbed the shovel. "Let me know when it's done. I got some digging to do."

* * *

He chose a spot near a grove of dogwood trees. The dirt was sandy, making the digging easy. The physical exertion was helping him calm down. It also tempered his grief of Martin's death. As he dug, he mentally reviewed his assets. He and Angela were in excellent condition to make the trip back to the fort. If she didn't want to return there, out of respect for his brother-in-law, he would take her to any place she could get transportation, as long as it was east.

He then brought the bodies to the graves and lowered them in. After covering them, Oli stepped back and wiped his forehead with his shirt sleeve. Removing the moccasins, he shook the sand out of them and headed back to the camp. The fire was down to smoldering coals. The remaining bacon lay in blackened strips soaking in grease. The biscuits looked okay but were now cold.

He poured a cup of the lukewarm coffee. He broke a biscuit open and put some greasy bacon between the pieces. Surprisingly, it wasn't too bad. After two more biscuits and another cup of coffee, he dumped the remaining grease onto the coals.

Angela sat staring at him as he ate. "We need to leave this place today. I have things packed and ready to be loaded on the horses."

"I still have to make a marker for Martin and say some words over the graves. I will also make one for Phillip if you want."

"It's a waste of time. The storms will wash them away within a few months and words won't help them."

"I wasn't asking." Feeling the anger coming back, he stuffed the remaining biscuit into his shirt pocket and went to get a piece of board from the wagon tailgate that had fallen away before the fire. He carved *Lt. Martin Maier* – July 1849. Placing the marker onto the grave, he stepped back. He looked toward the camp for Angela. She was loading gear on the two horses.

In the afternoon sun, he stood alone as he spoke over the men's graves. His throat ached as he finished. The truth was that he had known Martin only briefly. It was the sorrow he would be bringing back to Joan that choked him up.

Walking back to the camp, he saw that Angela was sitting on the black and had packs over the saddle on the bay. She was right about leaving the area. While the Cherokee seemed to have left, the danger of their returning was a real possibility.

"I am going back to Fort Leavenworth. The money is going with me. If you want, I will take you to another place that you can find transportation."

"I thank you for that, Oli." Her voice sounded odd.

"We will be taking turns riding and walking. You're mounted, so you can ride first." He then noticed that his rifle was in the saddle scabbard. He had set it against a windfall when making and placing the marker.

Moving to retrieve the weapon, Angela unexpectedly spurred the horses away from him. Turning them back, he was looking down the barrel of the shotgun and the coldest eyes he had ever seen.

"Stay away from that rifle," she warned. "Now, I want you to carefully remove your other gun and hang the holster on your horse's saddle horn."

Removing his revolver and holster, Oli kept his eyes on the shotgun-wielding woman. "You are making a mistake. I am not your enemy. I can take you away from here. Back to a town."

As he moved, she snapped at him, "Don't try anything! This load of buckshot will kill you and your horse."

Oli was in the company of an unstable woman. The loss of Martin and her brother must have made her snap. As he hung the holster on the bay, he wracked his brain for a way to make her realize that going on her own could result in her death.

Stepping back away from the bay, he watched her eyes for any change that would warn him that she was going to fire. He was close enough to her that the pattern would be tight. He still hoped he could reason with her.

"The Cherokee are still out there. Let me protect you from them. I will go wherever you want."

"You help me! My brother was right. You are a weak little man. I have food, water, and the money. The Mexicans are my friends. In a couple days I will be living like a queen. You, on the other hand will be feeding the vermin."

Her next move was clear as she grimaced, anticipating the recoil of the shotgun. Turning and throwing himself to the left, the weapon belched smoke and fire. At the same instant, he was hit with the shock and burning as the shot tore into his flesh. A piece of shot creased the back of his skull, sending him into a world of blackness.

CHAPTER FOURTEEN

There was a buzzing. What was it? Oli tried to look but he could not open his eyes. He tried to rub them, but his arms didn't work. He wondered where he was. Was he home in bed? What he could not see was the blood that had dried over his face and eyes from the skull wound. He was laying on his good arm, which was numb. The other had been hit by two pellets of buckshot. His mouth was open and in the dirt. The sun was coming up and the bluebottle flies had found him.

Bit by agonizing bit, consciousness returned and he pushed himself over using his legs. Rolling against the wounded right arm caused a wave of throbbing pain. His other arm began to tingle with pins and needles as the feeling returned.

He gasped from the pain and sucked some of the dirt into his mouth, resulting in spasms of coughing. This caused his head to pound from the wound. His eyes ripped open as he screamed in pain.

A shroud of darkness engulfed him again. Blessed, numbing darkness.

It was early afternoon before full awareness returned. He sat swaying. His mouth was dry. He needed to get to the stream for water. His wounded arm was useless. Any movement was too painful. His head still ached, but it was bearable. Using one of the windfalls for support, he slowly regained his feet.

Staggering from tree to tree, he worked his way toward the water. Once, he stumbled and laid for several minutes waiting for the aching in his arm to subside a little. Finally, at the stream he collapsed face-down in the water and struggled to raise his head enough to drink. Rolling over onto his back, he rested next to the water. Throughout the afternoon he took several drinks, attempting to rinse the dirt from his mouth each time. The life-giving water was helping to clear the fogginess in his head. He began to wash his wounds.

Sitting back against a willow tree, he regained some strength and balance. His stomach burned with hunger. He remembered the biscuit in his shirt pocket. It was crushed and damp. Eating it crumb by crumb helped a little.

* * *

Oli awoke, confused. Again, he wondered where he was. He attempted to move and the pain shot through his head and arm. He remembered being shot. He must have dozed off after eating the biscuit. He was sitting, slumped down against the tree. Carefully sitting up, he moaned as his stiff muscles rebelled. His wounds were a constant throb of pain.

He did his best to evaluate his injuries. While the head wound was sensitive, it was not that deep and had scabbed over. One of the arm wounds was an ugly, blue-green gash and would start bleeding with any movement. The other was a puncture wound and the lead shot was deep in the flesh.

Tenderly probing the arm, he could feel the pellet under the skin, opposite the wound. It had traveled through the muscle. This wound was his chief concern. It could have carried material from his shirt sleeve into the arm. If it took some cloth with it, there would be infection.

Tearing the sleeve off his shirt and cleaning it as best he could, Oli wrapped the wounds on his arm. The puncture wound had started to pound with the rate of his heart beat. He decided to spend the night next to the stream. He slept restlessly through the night. Nightmares of red-eyed wolves coming at him, and the aching in his arm, made it a long night.

He was sitting, awake, when light began to break in the east. He picked some plants and crushed them with the heel of the Good Knife. These he packed into the surface wound on his arm. He had no flint to start a fire. There was a piece in his pack, left up at the buttonbush patch. The first thing he needed to do was see if it was still there. In the past, he had learned how to make fire by rubbing wood together, but that took two good arms.

Taking another long drink, he then moved to the edge of the fortification that had protected them from the attacks. The hat of one of the men who owned the wagon was left hanging on a tree limb. He gently placed it onto his head, cocking it forward to keep the brim away from the wound. He found nothing else that he could use. Angela had taken pains to remove anything that would have helped him. With forced patience, he scanned the area before moving out.

The smell of death met him at the bush. The buttonbush flowers could not compete with the rotting bits of flesh left from Phillip's mutilation. Maggots crawled over a thick patch of blood and skin.

Relief flooded over him when he saw his pack and bow lying where he had left them. The ragged horse blanket would make nights more comfortable. Using the flint, he quickly had a fire going. He had fashioned a bowl out of willow bark. This he set next to the flames and warmed water. Much of the food he had been carrying was spoiled. Some nuts and berries were edible. He threw out most of the dried meat which had become damp and rotted. What little he had left was saved for later. Oli added the berries to the warm water for his meal.

With Martin dead, the drive to bring the payroll back to the fort was gone. He didn't care if he ever went back to Fort Leavenworth. He would travel east and stop at the first town he found. He would then find a way to get home after having the shot taken out of his arm.

He struggled to make another fish trap. He had a couple of arrows. The arm was becoming more difficult to use. He wondered if he could even use the bow. He hoped the traps would work. With a full belly, he would head out tomorrow.

By noon, he had his traps set in a slowly

moving pool in the stream. Sitting and drinking the warm berry broth while chewing on the last of his dried meat, he wondered what month it was. He had put July on the marker, but for all he knew it might be August.

With the best of luck, it would still take several weeks to travel to Elkader, Iowa. He wondered how Joan was doing. She must be getting large with child. Oli then worried, knowing all the things that could go wrong with a pregnancy. At this point, he wished that he had not gone after Martin.

After finishing his meal, he washed the arm wounds with warm water and put a poultice onto them. The area around the lead was hard and felt hot. He hoped that the infection would hold off long enough to get to a town. Even if he got to a doctor, chances were that the arm would have to be removed.

This thought made his mind wander back to Don Sikes, a dead man he had found in a cabin while lost in the wilderness some years back. Sikes had died after removing his own broken leg. Oli wondered if he would have the nerve to take his own arm off if it became badly infected.

The fish trap had two catfish. It was dark by the time he had them cleaned. The arm was aching and impossible to use. He had wanted to broil them and eat one that night, but he had no appetite. The pain was all-consuming.

There were some coals left from the fire. He put the fish next to the embers. If they were cooked by morning, he would try and eat. If they were still raw, he would have to throw them out. Taking the saddle blanket, he curled up on some willow leaves. He was very tired and felt hot. Keeping his arm over his head relieved the pain a little.

The night was cool, with the smell of rain in the air. Oli tossed and turned. He would be hot for a while, then there were chills. He woke to a gray and gloomy morning. It was full light, but he couldn't tell the time. The cloud cover hid the sun.

The smaller of the two catfish was fully cooked. The larger was cooked on one side and raw on the other. He ate what he dared of the larger fish. Then, filling his water bag and stowing the smaller fish, he left the area. The plan was to walk east on the Santa Fe Trail and hope to find a traveler headed the same way.

The rain came down in large drops an hour after he had started. Oli draped the blanket over his shoulders and continued. The rutted wheel track that he was walking in quickly turned from dust to mud. His ill-fitting moccasins were wet and slippery.

The rain lasted until midday. He was drenched and shivering. The arm continued to swell. The shirt sleeve had been used for a bandage. Sitting on a rock on the side of the trail, he examined the limb. He felt a large lump on the inner arm. It could be that the pellet was the source of the infection.

Exhausted after just the morning travel, he realized that something had to be done about the arm or all was lost. He had collected plants to pack the wound to help draw the infection out. It would only be helpful if he opened the arm.

Painstakingly, he collected fuel from several small bushes. The sun had burned through the hazy sky and was quickly making it hot and muggy. Every task took great effort, no matter how small. With the fire going he set the water bag down nearby, hoping it would warm somewhat.

He sat on the ground and put his arm on the rock. He had used the fire to clean the Good Knife's blade. Setting the knife down, he gingerly probed the arm. Locating what he hoped was the lead, he picked up the knife and placed the blade next to the spot.

The stress of what he was about to do made sweat break out on his forehead. Oli blinked rapidly to clear it from his eyes. The edge was sharp enough to shave with. Putting slight pressure with the knife, the point split the skin, creating a burning sensation. He continued to press until the blade was in about a half-inch.

The sting of the cut was much worse than the throbbing ache he had been putting up with. He took a moment to rest, blood running down the knife and over his hand. He knew what he was doing had to be done quickly, or he risked passing out and being no further ahead.

Drawing the knife down the arm about an inch, he could not prevent his reflexes from pulling the blade out. Feeling light-headed and nauseous, he slumped against the rock. His head fell against the infected arm and sent the pain up and down. He saw that the weight of his head on the arm had made the bleeding increase and included some pus.

Steeling his nerves, he carefully used the knife to search the new opening for the shot. Not finding it, it continued to gently press and massage the swollen arm. Bloody infection continued to drain. A second exploration with the knife found something hard that could be moved.

The searing pain forced him to stop several times before the lead pellet was removed. He continued to work the upper arm to try and drain it. With his left hand shaking uncontrollably, he tried to take the bandage with his poultice and wrap it over the cut. It took several attempts to succeed.

Weakness overtook him and he sat against the rock with his head hanging. He had hoped that the arm would feel better, but instead the cut had only added to the painful limb. He dozed fitfully for awhile. He woke with a ravenous thirst. His lips were split by the fever.

Grasping the water bag, he managed to untie it with his teeth and take a drink, spilling as much as he swallowed. The act of drinking tore at his parched throat. After taking several small drinks, his water bag was empty and his need for water remained. Tired and burning with fever, Oli slid sideways away from the rock and passed out.

CHAPTER FIFTEEN

There was the smell of smoke. Was it still a dream? Oli lay very still. His arm had stopped hurting. His eyes fluttered open. It was dark and he was warm. There was a flash of light and then a woman. An Indian woman was leaning over him. It had to be a dream. He closed his eyes tightly.

Something was pressed against his mouth and a warm liquid spilled down his cheeks. His eyes opened wide and he stared into the broad smile of an old woman. She was saying something he could not understand and trying to . . . feed him.

Opening his mouth, he let her pour the broth in. Hungrily, he swallowed and opened his mouth for more. After feeding him for a few minutes, she nodded and left, flipping down the flap on the way out. He was in a wickiup! An Indian lodge. Was he a prisoner? Moving his good arm, he noted that he was not bound. Another startling discovery was that he was naked under a buffalo blanket.

There was a bulky, crude wrap on his wounded arm. He moved it gingerly. There was still pain, but far less. He glanced around for his clothes. Nothing. His clothing was gone, as well as his pack. The truth was, neither was worth anything. But he was naked and had no way of leaving this lodge.

Sitting up, there was a brief wave of lightheadedness. After a moment, he dragged the buffalo blanket around his shoulders. He noticed the source of the smoke smell. A small fire pit in the center of the lodge had smoldering ashes. Next to the pit were items that appeared to be for doctoring his arm.

Again, the flap opened. A tall, handsome, young brave led the way in, followed by a stocky older man. At first glance, Oli thought he might have seen the younger man before.

The tall one tapped his chest and said, "Mahkateaa-mahweea."

The stocky Indian smiled and translated. "This is our chief, Wolf That Is Black, and I am Mahkwa-neemwa which is Bear That Watches. But call me Mika. We are of the Kickapoo tribe. He calls you Man Who Rides With Buffalo."

"It was you that I saved in the buffalo herd," Oli said to Wolf That Is Black.

Once again, the stocky brave translated. "He is the one that the buffalo attacked. We found you while coming back from a hunt. Some wanted to kill or just leave you. Our chief remembered you and your strong medicine. You were very sick. It has been five suns since we brought you here."

"I need my clothes and pack. My wife is with child and I must go back east."

"Your clothes were rags. We will bring you something to wear and a bow to hunt," he assured Oli. He then handed him the Good Knife and its sheath. "I have kept this for you."

Accepting the knife, Oli smiled. "Thank you, Mika, this knife has saved me many times. It is very strong medicine."

* * *

For the next two days, he was a guest of the Kickapoo. He was fed well and the old woman looked after his arm. It was still difficult to look at, but mobility had come back to the limb. The poultice she put on continued to draw the poison caused by the shotgun wound. He was given a nearly new set of buckskins, freshly treated with smoke to kill anything living in them.

He had learned that Mika had been a scout for both the U.S. Army and the Mexican Army. He was multilingual, speaking English, Spanish, some French, plus the languages of several tribes.

On the third day, Mika was translating a story being told around the council fire. It was interrupted by a commotion below, on a slope next to the village. Mika stood, looking toward the clamor.

Oli looked up. "Mika, what is it?"

"We have a scout watching the trail west. He has brought a man leading two horses."

Oli stood to look, but could not see above the others watching.

"The man is a friend of the Kickapoo. I know

him. We have scouted together."

"Is he a Mexican?" Oli asked.

"No, we call him, Miisiikwaaha, or Bull Buffalo. This man is very strong."

"What is his given name?"

"At the fort they call him Bart."

Oli ran forward, pushing through the crowd in front of him, forgetting about his wounded arm. Spotting the big man on horseback, he shouted, "Bart, over here! It's me, Oli."

Due to his weakened state, Oli was forced to stop, gasping for breath. The arm began to throb from being bumped. Bart looked up toward the running man who was calling his name.

"Is that you, Oli? Hey August, I have been looking for you," Bart shouted, swinging off his horse and running to meet his friend. "I thought you were dead. I found the graves. I was sure you were in one of the unmarked ones."

"I was almost killed by Angela. The Kickapoo saved me. Why . . . why are you out here?"

"As I said, looking for you."

"After what I said to you?"

Even though Bart towered over Oli, suddenly he looked small. Shaking his head, he said, "No, you were right. You depended on me and I chose a drink instead."

Before they could say anymore, the chief came down, welcoming Bart, and invited the two to join him near the fire. Some of the young boys took charge of the horses. For the first time, Oli noticed that one of the horses was his bay.

Following the chief, he was impatient to talk more with Bart, but out of respect he knew that he would have to wait. It was quickly apparent that Bart was well-respected by the Kickapoo. To Oli's surprise, they were conversing in the tribal language. His big friend was full of surprises. Mika kept him up on what was being discussed.

The shadows grew long in the Kickapoo village and the council fire reflected off the faces of the men sitting around talking. Cook fires had been lit and the smells of the evening meals filled the air. The old woman checked on the wounded arm, scolding Oli for being rough with it. The bandage showed more blood.

After she left, food was brought. The fare was bowls of buffalo meat, wild onions, and some kind of crunchy shoots. They ate using their knives or fingers. While the greasy gravy ran down their chins, the conversation continued. Oli listened more than spoke. He was anxious to get Bart away from the others to find out what had happened.

Finally, goodnights were said all around. Thanking the chief for his time, the two men went to check on the horses before heading toward the lodge. Both animals had been rubbed down and picketed on a good patch of grass.

"They have taken better care of our horses than their own," Bart observed as he patted the shoulder of his buckskin.

"My bay has lost some weight, but considering what Angela put it through, I guess I'm lucky it's alive."

"You're right there, my friend. She rode the black to death," Bart confirmed.

Glancing over at the pack horse, it was obvious that none of the attention had been given to it. He would give it a rubdown in the morning.

Sitting on a low rock ledge, Oli said, "Don't take this wrong, but what in the hell brought you out here?"

"Well, after you left me, I managed to stay drunk another week, or more, maybe. I was sleeping in the stable with my horse, eating seldom, and drinking too much. One morning, I woke up lying in the mud in front of the Oak Barrel. My face was bruised, there were knots on my head, a sour stomach had me on the verge of throwing up. Someone had emptied my pockets. I could hardly stand my own smell."

Bart stared at the ground, his face reflecting the memory of the distasteful experience. "I crawled more than walked into the saloon to try and beg a drink to settle my guts. The owner came around the bar with a short, lead-filled club. He cussed at me and said something about me being warned not to come back. It was lights out. I was in no shape to defend myself and took another one on the noggin."

"The next time I woke up, it was to the clatter of a metal tray being tossed down in the cell I was locked in. The smell of what was on the tray sent me into dry heaves. The next several days were hell. Between the shakes and sweats, I had plenty of time to think. Think about what you had said."

Uncomfortable with the things Bart was telling him, Oli interrupted, "I shouldn't have been so rough on you. I had just crawled through a ditch of filth, and took it out on you."

"No, I deserved what you said. By that time, eating regular and sleeping on the jail cot, helped me started thinking clearly. I began to realize I was wrong."

"About what? Drinking too much?"

"Well that too," Bart said, grinning, "but more important, about the robbery. I knew the lieutenant was your brother-in-law. I looked at all the evidence with one thought. Lieutenant Maier had to be innocent. I started going through what I had seen again. I did not like the conclusion, but it was that he had been involved. Maybe even Miss Russo."

"It was the next day when I was freed. The local law let me know that I was to leave the area before nightfall. I went straight to the major at the fort and told him my suspicions. I couldn't believe it, but he grubstaked me to go out and find the payroll."

"I was out of Fort Scott and looking for a trail well before dark. I ran across Mahkateaa-mahweea and his braves . . ."

"Ran into who?"

"The chief," Bart said, pretending to frown at being interrupted.

"Oh, I'm not used to hearing his name. Sorry, please go on."

"No problem. Anyway, I was told about you riding with the buffalo. They told me what direction you headed. I ran across the abandoned camp near the river. The weather had wiped out most of the tracks, but the wagon ruts were easy to follow. It joined up with the Santa Fe Trail and I was able to travel after dark. I now knew where you were headed."

"As I dogged the wagon, I finally came across tracks of your bay. I also found signs of Angela. I knew you must be with the lieutenant. I was sure I was getting close to the payroll. When I found the camp attacked by the Cherokee and saw the graves, I thought you lay under an unmarked one. The tracks leaving went west. You would have gone back to Fort Leavenworth. I knew Miss Russo and the lieutenant were in love. I figured she marked his grave before leaving."

"In my haste to follow her trail, I missed the sign of any other survivors, like you."

"You came upon an awful mess, Bart. It would have taken hours to sort it all out."

"You're too kind, Oli. The truth is I was focused on finding the money. Thinking you were dead, I made it my only goal."

"So, what happened to Angela and the payroll?"

"Like I said before, she ran the black to death. The bay, with all her supplies, was lost earlier while crossing a ravine. Maybe something spooked it, because it ran in the opposite direction, away from her. She chased it briefly and then gave up and headed back to find the Santa Fe Trail."

"She missed the road and ended up on the open plain. It looked like she panicked and ran the horse until it collapsed. I found her just beyond the horse. She was lying on the ground, curled up around the saddlebags holding the payroll. When the horse went down, she must have busted something inside. She was stone dead when I found her."

Oli thought about the cold eyes he had looked

into as she had shot him. "Her heart was evil. She turned Martin into a thief. She and her brother killed anyone they found inconvenient. I cannot feel bad about what happened to her."

"Well, my friend, she lies in a shallow, unmarked grave and will never hurt another person."

Realizing how late it had gotten, the two men headed for the lodge. Pulling back the flap, they entered to find Bart's gear neatly stowed. Surprisingly, next to Oli's blankets were a saddle and other stuff from the bay.

Crawling into his blankets, his mind going over all that Bart had told him, Oli laid there, unable to fall asleep. All of a sudden, he realized, Bart hadn't mentioned where he had put the payroll.

"Hey, Bart. Where is the payroll?" He doubted that he would have left it on the horses and let the Kickapoo move it.

After a brief pause, Bart responded, "I hid it before reaching their camp. I trust the Kickapoo and don't think they would take it or even look in our gear. But, I figured a little caution was a good idea."

* * *

For two more days the men were guests of the Kickapoo. Mika met Oli each morning right after the old woman checked his wound. Mika made sure that conversations were translated. Meals were plain, but filling. Their last night a fermented brew was shared. It was bitter to the taste, but quickly provided a pleasant glow.

The sun was up before Oli awoke. He had enjoyed a bit more of the brew than he should have. His head felt heavy. Looking over, he saw that Bart and his gear were gone. Startled, he dressed quickly and almost ran over the old woman as she came into the lodge with clean bandages.

He tried to convince her that he had to go find his friend. She would have none of his leaving before the wound was cleaned and rebound. The next couple of minutes seemed like an eternity as she washed and applied a poultice before wrapping the arm. Finished, she motioned him to go.

Hurrying from the lodge, he went to the area where the horses were kept. The bay raised its head and nickered at him. Bart's pack horse stood packed with the gear. The buckskin was gone. Mika saw him rushing down the hill and followed.

"You are looking for your friend?"

Not realizing Mika was there, the sound of the voice was a surprise. Turning quickly, he almost fell when his feet got tangled in some low brush.

"I didn't hear you come up. I was looking for Bart."

"He went for an early ride. Come, come with me and have some food."

Pausing a moment, he looked out on the grassy plain, before following Mika to the cook fire. They had finished eating before Bart came walking up the hill. He waved to them as he approached.

"I had an early errand before we left today, Oli," he said, sitting heavily next to the men and accepting a bowl from a young woman.

Setting his bowl down, Oli wiped his mouth with the back of his hand. "I should get my stuff together. I will be right back."

Mika offered to bring the bay to the lodge. It turned out that all his clothing was missing from his saddlebag except for a pair of long johns. His boots must have been discarded by Phillip.

Dressed in buckskins and a new pair of moccasins provided by the Kickapoo, he saddled the horse and stowed the gear. The buffalo blanket was left behind. His own blanket roll was still with the saddle.

CHAPTER SIXTEEN

Four days of hard riding brought the men to within sight of Fort Leavenworth. During the trip, Oli told Bart of his search for Martin, about finding the bodies of two of the robbers and of Angela's brother, Phillip. When he mentioned shooting the brave that used the yellow and black feathered arrows, a stunned looked crossed Bart's face.

"You killed Yellow Bird?"

"Was that his name?"

"He was a powerful Cherokee chief, ruthless in battle. He had the taste for slowly killing captives with fire."

"I buried the results of his method," Oli said, remembering the smell of meat roasting.

"That would explain why the Cherokee pulled out after Yellow Bird went down. With the great chief dead, they would think the attack was bad medicine."

He realized how lucky his quick shot had been as they rode. He thought about the men he had killed after leaving Elkader, the men he would have to atone for.

A shout from a small group of soldiers caught their attention. They rode out and flanked the two men. The senior man stopped in front of their horses. Oli recognized him as the man he had stuck with the Good Knife.

"Welcome back, Bart. I see you caught one of the murdering thieves?"

"No, corporal, this man was working with me to find the payroll."

Wheeling his horse around, he flung back, "I think the son-of-a-bitch was working with the lieutenant and that woman of his."

Surrounded by the soldiers, they were escorted into the fort and to the major's office. Dismounting, Bart grabbed the saddlebags off the pack horse.

"You can leave your gear on the horse. We will watch it for you, Nevell."

"Not these bags," Bart warned. "You boys watch the horses. Oli and I will bring these to the major."

Followed by a string of curses from the soldiers, the men entered the building. A young soldier in a clean, pressed uniform seated at the polished desk looked up at the visitors.

"Can I help you gentlemen?"

Dropping the heavy saddlebags onto the shiny desk, Bart said, "We're here to see the major."

The startled clerk stood quickly, knocking his chair over. "Get those filthy bags off my desk. You can't see the major today. He is preparing for a visit of some important people from Washington."

Snorting, Bart picked up the saddlebags. "Well, when you do see the major, tell him Bart Nevell and Oli August came by with the stolen payroll. We'll be up the street at the hotel."

As the men turned to leave, the clerk realized what they had said. "The payroll . . . ? Wait, don't go. I will inform the major."

In just moments, they were in front of the major. A half-smoked cigar was clenched in his teeth. His tightly fitting uniform gave the appearance that he was overweight. "My clerk said you have found the payroll?"

"Yes, sir," Bart replied. "It is all there, except a small amount. We think it was given to the Mexicans for safe passage through their territory."

Rolling the cigar from one side of his mouth to the other, the major asked, "What happened to the lieutenant and others that stole it?"

"They're all dead . . ."

Oli, unable to keep still, interrupted Bart. "Lieutenant Maier, uh . . . Martin died fighting Cherokee. He set up our defense, which allowed three of us to hold off a dozen hostiles."

A look of doubt crossed the major's face. Trying to help his friend, Bart added, "The Cherokee were led by Yellow Bird. In an exchange during close combat, the lieutenant took an arrow and the brave was killed."

"Yellow Bird dead?" the major said, obviously pleased with the news.

"Yes, sir, shot deader than hell, by the

lieutenant."

Oli listened in silence as Bart gave Martin the credit for the kill. If it would help at all with the way his brother-in-law was remembered, it was worth a little misinformation.

"I think the two people responsible for setting up the robbery were Phillip and Angela Russo."

"Miss Russo?" the major said, furling his brow. "How was she involved?"

"She was the one that convinced Martin to help with the robbery," Oli volunteered. "The plan started in New Orleans. She made Martin fall for her and made stealing the payroll a condition of staying together. She and her brother were the ones that killed during the theft and the escape." A wave of anger swept over him as he finally spoke what he believed.

The major seemed to have been only half-listening. He was looking over the gold and silver coins. Satisfied with what he saw, he called for the clerk to bring the new disbursing officer and some guards to his office.

Looking back at the two men standing in front of his desk, he said, "I must excuse myself now. Bart, sit down with my clerk and have him write down the details of the recovery. Mr. August, I thank you for working with my scout here. The clerk will provide you a chit to draw some boots and other clothing you might need. But before you do that, stop by our infirmary and have the arm looked at by Doc Calvin."

Turning to leave, Oli was stopped by an added comment from the major. "Having this payroll returned will make the visit from the people from Washington much more pleasant. And, Mr. August, I will enter the lieutenant's final acts in his record."

"Thank you, major," Oli replied, realizing that it was the most he could hope for.

The middle-aged Doctor Calvin was a stern-looking man. Oli sat on a low table, stripped to the waist, while the doc slowly removed the bandage from his arm. Once off the doctor sniffed the drainage on the bandage before tossing it into a tin bucket.

"I've seen worse," Doc Calvin said. "You say a Kickapoo woman cared for you?"

"That she did," the blond-haired man replied. "I can't tell you what she put to draw the bad stuff out, but it seemed to help."

"Looks like she done a little surgery opening the arm and getting the shot out," the doc observed. "You can thank her. It saved your arm and probably your life."

"I opened the arm up myself and got the buckshot out," Oli replied. "It's no doubt that her doctoring afterward saved me."

Ignoring the explanation, Doctor Calvin began to probe the partially closed wound, sending flashes of pain up the arm, causing Oli to involuntarily pull away. "You best hold still, or I'll have to tie the arm down or have someone come in here and sit on you."

Sweating and gritting his teeth, Oli endured the agony of the doctor's examination of the arm. Taking great care, Doc Calvin cleaned the wound and applied carbolic, which was another moment of hell for Oli. Before dressing the wound, he looked at the second arm wound and the head wound, which had both scabbed over.

Taking a seat near a small desk, the doctor said, "I want you to come and see me every day to have the wound looked at and a new bandage applied."

Oli stood up, grabbing his buckskin shirt. "I can't do that. I got a pregnant wife in Iowa and got to get back to her. I plan to leave tomorrow."

The doc picked up his pipe and walked over to the potbelly stove and using a short stick, he lit it. After a couple of draws, he blew a cloud of smoke toward the ceiling. "You can leave tomorrow if you want, but odds are you will be holding the new child with your one good arm. The Indian woman did her job and I plan to do mine," his face becoming sterner, if that was possible.

"Close attention is needed to prevent that arm from going sour," Doc Calvin warned. "I can't make you stay, but you'll be giving the arm no chance if you leave."

Paralyzed by indecision, Oli stood looking at the wise doctor. Then the doc continued, his voice kinder. "Are there folks back in Iowa that can help your wife if you aren't there?"

"There are," Oli replied.

"Then give the arm a chance," Doc Calvin said. "Even another week will make a lot of difference."

Nodding, Oli began to put the buckskin shirt on. "One more thing," the doctor said. "Get rid of the filthy shirt. I'll send someone out to get you some clean clothes."

Walking out of the infirmary with new long johns, a clean wool shirt and pants, Oli was still in need of some socks and boots. While the new clothing was itchy, it felt good to be properly dressed. He saw Bart coming out of the major's office.

Bart took the reins of their horses and led them up the street to meet Oli. "Damn army paperwork," the bruiser complained. "My hands' all cramped up from writing."

"I would have been happy to have traded cramped hands for what that doc put me through with the arm," Oli replied. "Now he says I have to stick around for a while so he can put me through some more torture."

Laughing, Bart looked down on his blond friend. "Doc Calvin is about the best you can find at any fort. If he says you should stick around, you best listen to him."

Digger was dozing in front of the livery, enjoying the summer sun. At the sound of the men coming towards him, he tilted his hat up and squinted at them. Recognizing Bart and Oli, he broke into a smile and rocked out of the old wooden chair.

"Let me take them animals for you," he said, "I got some morning coffee keeping warm on the stove. Just help yourselves."

While the hostler led the animals back to some stalls, Oli poured himself and Bart coffee. A quick sip told them that age had not helped to improve the morning coffee, but it was hot. Oli sat on a nail keg while Bart pulled over a stool.

"There was a reward for the payroll," the big man said.

"There was?" Oli asked, surprised.

"It ain't a fortune, but I figure we can split it,"

Bart said.

"That ain't necessary," the blond friend replied. "I was after Martin and was more than ready to let the payroll go."

"I kind of thought of us as partners and you earned your share," the bruiser replied.

Oli sat without replying as he nursed his coffee. Enough had been said and he would yield to Bart's wishes. Digger came back from putting up the horses and lifted the coffee pot, giving it a shake. "Just enough for one more cup," the hostler observed.

The two men left the livery and went to Ma Walker's boarding house. She broke into a smile when she looked up and saw Oli. "Welcome back," she said. "I got your special room available."

She then noticed Bart and the smile disappeared. "He can't stay here. He cost me three customers the last time he was here."

Trusting that his friend planned to stay sober, Oli prepared to defend him, when Bart spoke up. "Ma Walker, you don't have to worry. I was just making sure my friend got here without any trouble. I plan to stay in the barracks."

"It's a good place for you, with the rest of the rowdies," she replied.

Unaffected by her attitude, Bart smiled, "I'll meet you for breakfast if that's okay with the missus here."

Nodding, Ma Walker, replied, "If you're sober."

Again, Oli had the room at the end of the hall, including the red carpet. After stowing his gear under the bed, he sat down, remembering his last stay, which had been cut short by him climbing out the window ahead of some angry soldiers.

He looked down at the moccasins on his feet and decided that they looked out of place with his new clothing. It was about two hours before supper would be served, so he headed down the stairs and to the supply room to trade the chit for new boots and socks.

Sitting on a bench in the supply room with his new footwear, Oli carved an 'O' into each of the heels. There were a lot of similar boots at the fort and he wanted to make sure he had his marked. After pulling them on he stood, testing the fit with the new wool socks. They were a bit tight, but a few days of wearing should stretch them out.

Ma Walker had roasted a buffalo tenderloin for supper, along with beans and greens. She also had a berry pie for dessert. A couple of men who were traveling with the men from Washington were staying at the rooming house and took their meals there.

Oli kept to himself during the meal and overheard their conversation. It appeared that the meetings with the major had gone well. The return of the payroll was one of their topics, but nothing was said about those who had robbed the money. Word was out about Angela Russo's part in the robbery and Oli's wondered what the table conversation in the stately white house was like this evening.

With the meal finished, Oli felt restless. It was dusk outside and a breeze was blowing, taking away the heat of the day. He needed a walk to help stretch out the new boots. Thanking Ma Walker for the fine meal, Oli walked toward the river.

In the morning he would send a telegram to Joan. As he walked, Oli pondered what he would include. He'd like to say that he was well and he'd be home in a couple of weeks, but something would have to be said about Martin. The telegraph was expensive and anything he sent would have to be short.

Arriving at the pier, Oli took a seat on one of the pillars. The breeze caused waves to lap against the shore. Just north of him were two steamboats moored, with smoke rising lazily out of their stacks into the moonlit sky.

Everything around him was at peace, safe in the shadow of the fort. He thought about how the fight with the Cherokee had been just a week west of here, and beyond there was trouble with Mexico. Oli was thankful to be going back to a place where he wouldn't have to look over his shoulder and worry about what might appear in the night.

Still without an answer about what he was going to send to Joan, Oli headed back toward the boarding house. The boots had a bit more bite as his feet began to get sore. He decided that a walk each evening would be needed to make them comfortable.

Good to his word, Bart joined him for breakfast. He had a bag of coins, which was Oli's share of the reward. The two men from Washington had left earlier on one of the steamboats. Ma Walker served them eggs with slices of leftover roast. She also had biscuits and jam made from the same berries as the pie the prior night.

Bart was in good spirits. The army wanted him to stay and scout for them. There had even been talk of him becoming regular army. "There is a good chance you might end up spending a lot of time in the stockade if you got a hold of a bottle," Oli warned him.

"That is something to consider," Bart replied. "Even then, I would eat regular and have a roof over my head."

"I believe I'm going to have a bath before going to see the doc today," Oli said. "It might even help to take some of the stiffness out."

"While you're getting nice and clean," Bart replied, "I'll be heading with a crew about an hour west. A herd of buffalo was spotted and the army needs some meat."

Ma Walker directed Oli to a barber and bath. He walked toward the place, looking forward to a good soak. Lounging in front of the saloon were two off-duty soldiers. Oli recognized the tall, red-faced man he had stuck with the Good Knife. The other was the ruddy-faced man he'd had words with before.

"I don't know what kind of lies you told the major," the tall soldier said, "but I believe you should be hung in that no-good lieutenant's place."

Oli was tempted to stop and set the man straight, but the two troublemakers against him with a bad arm would be poor odds. He also noticed that the tall one was wearing his dragoon on his hip. As the two men continued to sling insults at him, Oli continued toward the bath. "Today is not the day to settle up," he mumbled to himself.

Bart was gone on the hunt for three days. Each day Oli want to Doctor Calvin's and had his arm worked on. Each visit brought good news of improvement. The arm remained stiff and tender to the touch, but the wound was closing nicely.

On the way out of the doctors, Oli ran into Bart. The bruiser was just back from the hunt and they brought in three buffalo. Seeing his friend, the big man said, "I see you got yourself a new Colt-Paterson."

"With one arm almost useless," Oli replied, "I figured I'd best get one to even up the odds on some of the surlier soldiers."

"It was probably a good idea," Bart said. "There are those that figure you got away with helping your brother-in-law."

"Well, the doc figures I'll be able to travel in the next few days and I will be far from all of this, and I don't really care what they think," Oli replied, feeling a little anger.

"It's a wise move," Bart agreed. "Some of these hammerheads will never see the truth."

Heading back toward the boarding house, Oli bid goodbye to his friend. While he had said that he didn't care what they thought, the truth was that it bothered the blond man a lot. A man's word was important, and having others think that he was less than honest was maddening. The only solution was to confront the accusers and, if necessary, kill them. Oli shook his head. There would be no more killing.

After supper, Oli was back on the street. His daily walks were breaking in the boots just fine. He found that sitting at the pier brought him comfort. In three or four days he would be catching one of the steamboats and heading home. Joan had acknowledged his telegram and wished him a safe trip home. She had said nothing about Martin's death.

His thoughts were about his family as he walked back to the boarding house. He flexed the injured arm. While still far from normal, it did feel better each day. All of a sudden, two men stepped out of the shadows. In the low light of the street, Oli knew that it was the two soldiers. He could see that they were both carrying sidearms.

In a calm voice, Oli asked, "Can I help you gentlemen?"

The men were just over 20 feet from Oli. The night breeze brought the smell of rye on the men. The taller one said, "We come to settle with you for the two friends of ours that was killed by your thieving brother-in-law."

"Martin is dead," Oli replied. "He paid for what he did. There was nothing I could have done to change anything that happened."

"You're a liar," the ruddy-faced man said.

"I am sorry you feel that way," Oli said. "Now, I need you to decide which one of you is going to die. I can't kill both of you before you get me, but I will surely kill one of you. Which will it be?"

"What?" the tall one said.

"You heard me," Oli replied. "My knife will kill one of you. Choose!"

From behind them came a voice. "He is right. I seen him with the knife. Choose carefully, because I will kill the one that he doesn't."

The large hulk of Bart stepped out of the shadows. Oli snapped, "Stay back, Bart! This is my fight."

The two men held their hands well away from the dragoons. "We didn't mean nothing," the ruddy-faced man said. "I only meant it's hard to . . ."

"Nobody got to die here," the tall man interrupted. He had felt Oli's knife before and was now shaking.

"Drop your guns and get the hell out of my sight," Oli growled.

"Were doing it," the ruddy-faced man said. "Don't stick us with that knife."

As their dragoons hit the dirt, the two men turned and ran down the street, into the shadows.

Oli walked down the street toward the boarding house. Bart came alongside. "You handled that just right."

"I think they were more afraid of you behind them," Oli replied.

"I don't see why," Bart said. "I didn't even have a gun."

While his stomach was still tight from the confrontation, Oli couldn't help but smile.

CHAPTER SEVENTEEN

The next morning Oli delivered the two dragoon guns to the major's office. The two men would have a difficult time explaining how they had lost them. The visit to the doctor had gone well. Oli was told he could head for home as long as he promised to see the doctor in Iowa once he got there. Anxious to see his family again, Oli made arrangements to leave the following day.

The next morning was brisk, with the horse's breath creating plumes of steam in the late summer air. The two men stood in the muddy street, wishing each other safe journey.

"Again, I want to thank you for sharing the reward money with me," Oli said.

"Like I said, we were partners in this, Oli. You would have done the same for me. Besides, this way you can ride the rivers back to Iowa."

Adjusting the itchy clothes, Oli smiled at his friend. "You mentioned at breakfast that you weren't going to stay with the army. Where are you heading, Bart?"

"Texas, I guess. There is a little lady I met down there that promised to wait for me if I ever decided to settle down. I plan to use my share of the reward to buy a small ranch. Maybe raise some horses and a few cows."

Giving the big man a firm handshake, Oli felt sad, knowing that this was probably the last time he would see his friend. "If you and the lady ever decide to travel, you are always welcome in Elkader."

The sound of the boat whistle broke the moment and both men mounted their horses, with Bart riding south leading a pack horse and Oli heading for the landing on the river.

The bay was led onto the steamboat and put in its stall. He gave the hostler a little more money for extra grain. The trip home would take a week and the horse would be in good shape when they reached Elkader.

After taking care of the horse's needs, he went to his stateroom to stow his gear. He shared a room with three other men. None were in the room, so he chose an empty bunk and put his stuff under the bed. Carrying his valuables in his new money belt and with his Colt-Paterson in his waist band, he headed out to find some supper.

The panting of the steam engine was a constant presence on the boat as black smoke belched out of the stacks. Sitting at the rail, Oli stared at the water churning around the flat, broad hull. The comfort he had felt when the major had said a mention of Martin's final acts would be put into the permanent record had waned. It had been replaced by the thought of having to tell Joan about her brother's involvement in the stealing of the payroll. He thought about the telegram. He had wanted to tell her more, but the cost and other limitations of the telegraph had made it impossible.

Turning to watch a floating tree scrape against the side, he bumped his arm. It was still tender, causing him to wince. Between the army doctor and the Kickapoo woman, the wound was well on the way to healing. The doctor had warned him that he would probably never have full strength in the arm.

On the third day, Oli had to change boats in St. Louis. He had a six-hour wait and he rode the bay through the streets. He was surprised at the changes since he had been there last. The city had grown and spread out. The area where he had met Albert's wagon train was now built up with factories. Like before, the pier was still loaded with goods coming to and going from the port.

He was glad once he had his horse loaded onto the new steamboat. He was now on his last leg of the way home. Again, he shared the stateroom with four others. One of the men in his stateroom was a young lawyer who liked to gamble. Oli ate his supper with the man. As they finished the young man urged Oli to join him at the tables. He had a system that he offered to share, which would assure him of a winning night. While he liked the man's enthusiasm, the thought of risking hard-earned money did not appeal to Oli. Later, the young lawyer came into the stateroom, rather subdued after a losing night.

The boat would arrive at a Mississippi landing a half-day's ride from Elkader. Oli's dark mood grew the closer he got to home. He knew that Joan deserved the whole truth. He was not sure that he could cause her the pain that the truth would bring.

Worry was heavy on his face. There was little to do on the boat if you weren't drinking or gambling. Unlike the young lawyer, he knew that card sharks worked the boats. The share that he had gotten from the reward would be needed when he got home. Without him being there, more of their winter food would have to be purchased.

To help keep his mind busy, he pampered the bay. It had been brushed and groomed more than it had ever seen in the past, and no doubt in the future. His original saddle had been lost when Phillip had left him. The saddle the horse came back with needed repair and cleaning. He also modified it to fit better.

He checked and re-checked his gear. A new slicker was among the items he had gotten from the army supply. He made notes in the tally book about things concerning the trip. He spent time designing and planning some things, like the porch.

The night before the landing he got little sleep. It seemed long ago when he had left to help Martin. He thought about being back home and seeing his family. The new baby would be here soon. Also, the burden of having to tell his wife about her brother's guilt weighed on him. It was impossible to turn his thoughts off.

He was readying his horse when the boat bumped against the landing. The sun had just come up. The door used to offload stock slid open. Oli was temporarily blinded by the bright sunshine. He led the horse down the wooden ramp, shading his eyes.

Cargo was being brought ashore on a second stage plank. Freight wagons waited to be loaded. Boldly marked on several boxes and barrels was Wolf Bros. Memories of the man they had sent to follow him came back, adding to his dark mood.

Oli left the landing with the bay at a trot. By midday he would be back in Elkader. He played over and over through his mind what he was going to say to Joan. Each time he changed it a bit to try and make the words just right.

As he got closer, the smell and the feel of the area became more and more familiar. His mood rose and fell by the minute as it went from excitement to worry. As he reached the Turkey River, Oli stopped to water the horse. He led it under an oak tree to check the saddle cinch. There were footsteps crunching on the gravel behind him.

"I see you found your way back home from the west," a sarcastic voice said.

Turning, he was face-to-face with Jacob Wolfe. "Is this your new job, to be present when I leave or return to Elkader?"

"Did you actually go see your thieving brother-in-law, or was it for more gold?"

Anger raced through Oli's veins. Throwing down the bay's reins, he stepped up to Jacob. "Don't you ever speak of Martin that way."

"Don't threaten me, August. Haven't you learned that by now?"

Even though Jacob was much larger than Oli, the strain of the trip had him wound to the breaking point. Grabbing the bigger man by the coat, he pulled him close and kicked his feet out from under him. The two of them fell heavily to the ground, with Oli on top. The Good Knife appeared in his hand and the razor-sharp blade was against Jacob's throat, drawing a fine line of blood.

"I've learned a lot, Jacob. On this past trip, I learned about killing, starting with the man you sent to follow me. You know what? I am quite good at it."

Pushing himself away from the startled man, he stood over him, staring into fear-filled eyes. "You and I both have to live in this town. You and your brother are good businessmen and the town needs you. My plan is to make a comfortable home for my wife and children. The place is big enough for all of us."

Turning, he caught up the bay's reins and swung into the saddle. Leaving Jacob lying on the ground, he rode away towards home. He was surprised at how he felt. The strain of the trip was gone. The confrontation with Jacob had released the tension. Even the ache in the injured arm felt good. Thinking clearly, he now knew what had to be told to his wife.

As he approached his house, he felt his heart beating faster. Coming around the end of the building, he saw Joan hanging clothes. Her stomach was large with child. Young Karl was handing her wet items from the basket. Jenny sat playing with a rag doll.

Seeing his father riding up, Karl squealed. Dropping the wet clothes onto the ground, he ran as fast as his little legs would carry him toward his father. Sliding off the horse, Oli scooped the young lad up and hurried to the open arms of his loving, bride.